Famous for Thirty Seconds

COMMERCIAL BREAKS

Famous for Thirty Seconds

BY P. G. KAIN

ALADDIN M!X

NEW YORK   LONDON   TORONTO   SYDNEY   NEW DELHI

ALADDIN M!X
Simon & Schuster Children's Publishing Division
1230 Avenue of the Americas, New York, NY 10020
First Aladdin M!X edition March 2012
Copyright © 2012 by P. G. Kain
All rights reserved, including the right of reproduction in whole
or in part in any form.
ALADDIN is a trademark of Simon & Schuster, Inc., and related logo
is a registered trademark of Simon & Schuster, Inc.
ALADDIN M!X and related logo are registered trademarks
of Simon & Schuster, Inc.
For information about special discounts for bulk purchases, please contact
Simon & Schuster Special Sales at 1-866-506-1949
or business@simonandschuster.com.
The Simon & Schuster Speakers Bureau can bring authors to your live event.
For more information or to book an event contact the Simon & Schuster Speakers
Bureau at 1-866-248-3049 or visit our website at www.simonspeakers.com.
Designed by Karina Granda
The text of this book was set in Bembo.
Manufactured in the United States of America 0212 OFF
2 4 6 8 10 9 7 5 3 1
Library of Congress Control Number 2011922714
ISBN 978-1-4169-9786-3 (pbk)
ISBN 978-1-4169-9789-4 (eBook)

For my love, WBC,
from whom I never need a break,
commercial or otherwise

ACKNOWLEDGMENTS

First, I would like to thank every casting director who ever kept me waiting for a commercial audition long past my appointment time. If it weren't for you I would never have thought of writing this book.

One of the great joys of writing a book is the opportunity to recognize the people who help you along the way. So thank you, Rebekah and Meline, for helping me figure out when food is spoiled; Pam for being the best start to my day; Carley for being at the intersection of every part of my life with love, fun, and unconditional support; Taylor for being my book BFF, making writing fun, and calling me a hundred times a day; Chris for keeping me from level B; Loins for loinsabrating; Mad for being a fellow two; Sarah for conversations in my head; Shari for reminding me of who I am; Beth for knowing me as long as I have known myself; Julia for guidance; Kate, Lyn, and Greta for making the 17th floor a family; Olivia for putting the "fun" and "friend" into FFiR; Virgil for help with Chinese; and my family, Judi and Matt, for a lifetime of humor, support, and love.

Thank you, William, for being my first reader, first respondent, and first in my life.

I would like to thank the parents of my agent, Alyssa Eisner Henkin, for making her the middle child. She claims her middle-child identity makes her the calm, supportive force she is, but I know her grace goes well beyond her birth order. Thank you, Kate Angelella, for acquiring this series. I truly appreciated our time together. Thank you, Fiona Simpson, for adopting this project and making it your own. I admire your patience, creativity, and hair.

As an author of books for young readers, I have met so many wonderful librarians, and I want to thank them for their support and for helping me make a connection with my readers. Librarians are the casting directors of reading, in a good way. I look forward to continuing to work with you!

Most important, I want to thank YOU. Yeah, you: the kid who loves to read so much you're actually reading the acknowledgments. That's amazing. Thanks for reading this book. I'd love to hear from you, so please stop by my website, www.TweenInk.com, or send me an e-mail at pg@tweenink.com so I can thank you personally.

CHAPTER 1

You know me.

You don't know *how*, but you definitely know me.

You don't know that I've studied ballet since I was six or that I once failed the same spelling quiz three times in a row, but you know me. You see me trying on a pair of sneakers at the mall or talking on my cell phone outside of school and you think, "Did that girl go to summer camp with me?" or "Is that the girl who went out with my cousin?"

I didn't and I'm not.

If you've ever eaten a *Gotta Have It* candy bar then you've either put your pinkie on my nose or pressed your thumb across my forehead. If you sat through an entire episode of a popular reality show last year then, in between the screeching of your favorite pop songs, you've seen me enthusiastically taking pictures of my friends at the beach with my brand-new Globaltel cell phone camera. If you've turned on your television at all over the past decade, opened a single magazine, or walked through a supermarket—or even a well-stocked *mini-mart*, then you know me.

Up until last year I booked more television commercials and print jobs than any other girl in my agency. From before I can remember, I have been a top earner for The A-Lister Agency. Judith List herself discovered me when I was six months old.

Judith ran into my mother. Literally. My mother was driving us to a "Mommy and Me" class so she could have some one-on-one time with me while my older sister Christine was with a sitter. But suddenly it was one-on-one-*on-one* when Judith accidentally hit my mother's bumper. When Judith came out to inspect the damage she saw me gurgling in my car seat.

My gurgle was the *exact* gurgle ad companies were looking for at the time. Two weeks later I'd beaten out dozens of other babies to become THE face of Good Baby formula. My mother says I was too young to be able to remember anything about the shoot, but I swear I have a very specific memory of being in front of all these cameras and lights and a studio *full* of people focusing their attention on me—and how they might make my naturally adorable baby smile adorable times ten with the right camera angle.

My life had been a steady stream of school, callbacks, and bookings . . . up until last year. A few days after my twelfth birthday my mother told me The News.

The News basically took my life, tore it into little pieces, and then forced those pieces to live in Hong Kong for a full *year*. I have repeated this torn-paper image to my mother many times and what does she tell me? I am being "overdramatic." I assure you, if anything, I am being *under*dramatic.

"Brittany," my mom told me the night she shared The News, "it's only *one* year. It's not like we're selling the house! The paper just needs someone to cover the Hong Kong bureau for twelve months then we'll all be back in New York. When I told Christine, she was excited."

Of course Christine was excited. As long as she can take her soccer ball with her, she has something to do and an instant collection of friends. But even though we look so much alike we could be twins and she is a mere fifteen months older than I am, we are about as different as sisters can be.

Christine has *it*—that thing that makes people just automatically want to be friends with her. Everyone *always* likes Christine. Even me. I adore her. Sometimes I feel like she is the one person I can just be myself around. She's just one of those people who has so much confidence being herself that she makes *other* people comfortable with who *they* are. Christine's total lack of interest in popularity makes her even more popular. To her, Hong Kong was just another place to make a new start with new friends. To me, it was The End.

"It will be fun," my mom said with a little too much enthusiasm.

I looked at her in shock like she had three heads and one of them was put on backward. A year in Hong Kong? While I am at the height of my commercial career? Right after I'd gotten a second callback for a new foaming face soap? My mom must have been able to tell what I was thinking because she tried to offer a counter argument:

"Brit, won't it be nice to take a break from all your look-sees?" she asked. "You work too hard."

"Mom!" I shouted. "For like the ga-billionth time, they are called GO-sees! An audition for a print job is a *go-see*. I've only been doing this since I was in diapers."

"But that's exactly my point. You'll get a whole year to enjoy just being a normal kid."

There is absolutely nothing I enjoy about being a *normal kid* and I was as sure of this on day one as I was on day 365. (Yes. I actually marked off each day with a big, black X on a wall calendar next to my bed.)

I never stopped missing the excitement of getting an appointment for a commercial that would air during the Super Bowl *or* the way I felt when my face would pop up on a package of cookies at the local Stop & Shop.

Approximately one week before we had our flight scheduled to return home to New York, I called Judith to tell her that my stupid mother's stupid job in stupid Hong Kong was about to finish and that I was ready to get back in the game.

Christine sleeps for almost the entire flight except the hour or so we play cards and when she listens to me make fun of the food served during the flight. (Tuna lasagna? Seriously?) I am too excited to sleep for even a second. Every moment that passes takes me farther away from Hong Kong and closer to my big comeback. Instead of napping, I actively daydream about the spots I'll book and what magazines I will be seen in. I wonder if I'll book my first go-see right away!

After a year of being away from all of it, tomorrow I finally make my return. Judith asked if I could come into her office at the agency the morning of my first day back. I guess she's just as excited as I am to start booking her top-earning client. I could be out on an audition the very next day!

As Flight 792 from Hong Kong makes its final approach to JFK International Airport, the plane tilts gently so the entire Manhattan skyline is slowly revealed as the early summer sun sets. My heart almost jumps out of my chest and I think, *if I had a parachute I would jump out right now.* I remind myself that my old life is less than forty-eight hours away.

I draw a calming breath in through my nose and let it out through my mouth as I take a closer look at the skyline. I expect it to greet me like an old friend and, while most of it is the same, there are parts I don't recognize at all. A number of new glass skyscrapers have been put up over the past year, some still in the middle of construction. It's amazing how much can change in a year.

For a brief moment I think maybe this is something I should worry about, but then I put the thought out of my mind and focus on the gentle descent of the plane. The world may have changed but I am still me, and what's important is that you still know me.

You *do* still know me . . . Don't you?

CHAPTER 2

The morning of my meeting with Judith, I visit four of my very best friends before I even go downstairs for breakfast. It's been a full year since I've seen Priscilla, Jean, Margaret, and Kate and I want to make sure nothing has happened to them. As soon as I am done showering and doing my hair, I decide to see how they are. I walk over to the white chest of drawers that I painted roses and daffodils on one day after a particularly inspiring HGTV program and open the top drawer. There they are, my old friends. The four shirts that have gotten me through almost every go-see, audition, and callback I have ever been on.

When Judith calls with an appointment for a go-see, she usually includes a brief description of the "type" they are looking for. Each director thinks they are looking for something totally unique but I've found that each description boils down to four major types, and I've managed to find the right top for each type and have named them accordingly.

There is a pink chiffon blouse with small pearl buttons down the front and ruffles on the shoulders that I call Priscilla. She's the girlie-girl that you see on the cover of magazines or in some goofy sitcom that loops endlessly on the Disney Channel. She has tons of girlfriends, talks endlessly on her cell phone, is most likely to be involved in cheerleading or planning the school dance. You'll see me in Priscilla at go-sees for makeup lines, spas, or any health-and-beauty related product.

Right next to Priscilla is my dear friend Margaret. Margaret is a straight-A student and also class president. You'll find her seated in the front row of every class. Margaret is a no-nonsense, light blue button-down shirt with three-quarter sleeves that could double for a school uniform in a pinch and often needs to. Margaret is worn at go-sees for office-supply chains, technology products, and anything that has to do with school or education.

Jean is the outdoorsy gal who is kind of a tomboy. She's not afraid to get dirty and when she goes to the beach she is there to swim in the ocean or play volleyball. You'll see her at go-sees for anything related to sports or gym class. She is a red and white, wide-striped tank top with wide shoulder straps.

Then there is Kate.

Kate is my go-see go-to girl. You'll basically see her everywhere at go-sees for everything. She is funny but not obnoxious, pretty without being intimidating, and smart without being boring. She can stand out in a crowd and also blend in when she needs to. Kate's secret is that she is a simple, three-button polo shirt in a unique shade of teal.

As soon as I see Kate, I know she is the perfect choice for my meeting with Judith and my return to the commercial world. I take Kate out of the drawer. The piqué teal fabric floats down my arms and over my head, but then it stops. For a second I'm not sure what is going on so I just tug at the edge of the shirt to get it on, and after a few pulls the rest of the shirt comes over my head. But for some reason it doesn't feel the way it used to. I walk over to my bedroom mirror to examine myself.

Something is definitely off. Usually the front of Kate hits me just below my belt buckle, but today she sits almost above the top edge of my jeans and she is really, *really* snug under my arms.

"Brit! Hurry up!" my mother yells from downstairs. "We have to drop Christine off at soccer camp before we catch the train. You don't want to be late for Judith. Are you ready?"

"I'm coming!" I shout back. Then it dawns on me. Someone must have washed Kate in very hot water while I was gone and she shrunk or something. I suddenly remember a teal shirt that I bought online while we were in Hong Kong. It's only a cheap imitation of Kate—more of a Katie Jo—but with my mom already worried about missing the train, Katie Jo is going to be as good as it gets. I look furiously for the piece of luggage that is keeping Katie Jo hostage and release her from imprisonment. I throw her on and look in the mirror. I hate to change any part of my system, but Katie Jo will have to represent today. I don't have any other choice.

I finish getting ready as fast as I can, race downstairs, and throw a granola bar in my bag before meeting my mom and Christine in the car.

I organize my folder of headshots and résumés on my lap while Christine bounces a soccer ball on hers. "What's your go-see for?" she asks, wrapping an elastic around her ponytail.

"I don't have a go-see today. I have to meet with Judith first," I tell her and help her with her hair.

Our blond hair is the exact same color and almost the same length, but Christine's is cut to endure long soccer matches whereas mine is cut for versatility. I need it to *look* like it might endure a long soccer match, but I also need to be able wear it so it *looks* like I am going to a school dance or *looks* like I am hanging out on the beach. It's much easier to make your hair actually do one thing rather than make it *look* like it's doing a bunch of different things.

"Are you excited to see your old friends?" I ask. The only thing that bothered Christine about being in Hong Kong was not being able to hang out with her friends in Great Neck. Of course, now that she is back, she misses all the friends she made in Hong Kong.

"Sure. Are you excited to see all your friends when you have your first audition?" she asks.

"Sure," I say quietly and without enthusiasm. I've tried to explain it to Christine before but she never seems to quite get it. The other girls at the go-sees and auditions are not exactly my friends. I've known a lot of them since I was a little kid, and I probably spend as much time with them as Christine does with her teammates—but I wouldn't call these girls my friends. The truth is, I book more spots than anybody else. It's hard to make friends with the other girls when you're taking away the very thing they want.

Everyone is polite and friendly on the surface, but I'm sure most of the girls were thrilled when I left because it gave them more opportunities. I hope a lot of these girls have something to fall back on because, now that I am back, I have every intention of regaining my number-one status.

We drop Christine off at soccer camp and then head to the train station. The train from Great Neck to Penn Station only takes thirty-five minutes and my mom talks on her cell phone the entire ride. She only stops when we enter the tunnel that takes us under the island of Manhattan into the actual center of the universe.

Unable to terrorize her assistant via cell phone any longer, my Mom turns her attention to me. "Now Brittany, just because your father and I have decided you are old enough to handle your auditions and go-sees on your own for the time being doesn't mean we won't change our minds. If we find out you aren't following the rules, then it's back to having your father or me as a chaperone."

I just listen and fight the urge to roll my eyes at her. Even the slightest backward movement of my pupils might cause my mom to change her mind about letting me fly solo, so I make sure that I keep them absolutely level.

As soon as the train doors open, everyone rushes out to the platform and up the stairs. My mother grabs my hand and weaves us through the orchestrated chaos. Usually I hate letting her control me, but in this case I'm grateful to let my mind wander as she guides me through the mass of people up to street level.

"Now, Brittany, you are to call me if . . ."

"Mom," I tell her, making sure there is no trace of a "tone" in my voice, "I know. Call you if there is so much as a crack in the sidewalk. I'm just going to see Judith."

"Fine. Make sure you tell Judith and everyone else in the office hello from me. I'll see you for lunch. Just be careful and . . ."

"I know," I say, preempting her. "*Call* you."

"Actually, I was going to say have fun." She gives me a quick hug and goes up Seventh Avenue to her office near Times Square.

I start walking down the familiar, happy path, toward the Flatiron area and Judith's office. The building where her office is located is a tall, dark, glass skyscraper on the east side of Madison Square Park. It towers over most of the other buildings, and when I was a kid I thought that was because it was the most important. I walk past the front desk in the lobby and head toward the bank of elevators designated for floors twenty through thirty-five.

I stare at the sign on the door to the office suite before opening it. It reads, THE A-LISTER AGENCY. JUDITH LISTER, AGENT. Everything I want begins on the other side of this door. For a second I feel like Dorothy in *The Wizard Oz* the moment before her life goes from black-and-white to color.

CHAPTER 3

I open the door to Judith's office and Peggy gets up from her desk and shouts, "Doll, you're finally back!" Peggy is somewhere between seventy and three thousand years old. She's been Judith's assistant since the dawn of time. She is actually shorter than me—and thinner—but the last thing in the world you would call her is frail. She's more like a small jet-propelled missile.

Peggy's Brooklyn accent is as thick as the rising humidity outside. When I was a kid I used to think that callbacks were called cawbacks because Peggy would leave a message on our voice mail saying, "Brit'knee's got a cawback tom-aura . . ."

"Hi, Peggy. Great to see you," I say and give her a hug. I look around the office suite and very little seems to have changed. I find this comforting. There are still the same chairs in the reception area.

The two doors behind Peggy's desk lead to the agent offices. The bigger one is Judith's and the smaller office belongs to Marcus—her subagent who handles mostly adults.

The door to Marcus's office is open and I wave to him and he waves back even though he is on the phone. Of course, behind Peggy's desk is a larger-than-life-size poster from the Tastytime campaign I did when I was seven. I'm sucking on a drink box and smiling while giving a thumbs-up sign. That was one of my first big campaigns.

"Oh, gosh," I say. "You still have that old thing up?" I ask, pointing to the poster.

"Old thing?" Peggy asks with mock offense. "Your Tastytime campaign is what built this agency. Judith says that poster reminds her of one of the very first big campaigns that put this agency on the map."

"That's sweet," I say, trying to sound as gracious as possible.

At that moment the door to Judith's office opens and in the doorway is none other than Judith herself, looking as Park Avenue as always. "There's my girl," she says, walking toward me, but then she pauses. "Wait," she says, "turn around." Her fingers move in a circle in the air.

I smile for a second and then twirl around slowly so that Judith can get a good look at me.

"Phew!" she says in a way that I can't tell if she is kidding or not. "I was a little worried that after a year in Hong Kong you would come back with half your hair dyed blue and the other half shaved off."

"Nope," I say as I raise my shoulders to my ears and plaster the same smile on my face that I have in the Tastytime drink poster. "I'm still exactly the same."

"Well," Judith says, "not *exactly* the same." She opens the door to her office and says, "Peggy, hold all my calls while I get reacquainted with my favorite client."

Before I can say anything, Peggy chimes in, "Oh she says that to all her clients."

"That's true Peggy but when I say it to Brittany, I actually mean it." We all laugh and I follow Judith into her office.

Judith takes her usual seat behind her desk and I sit in the chair across from her, where I can gaze out the window to the incredible view of downtown Manhattan. For the first ten minutes or so we make small talk. Judith wants to know all about Hong Kong—the food, the sights, the people. I have absolutely no interest in talking about Hong Kong, but

I realize that she is only being nice, so I tell her a few stories about ancient temples, noodles with fresh ginger, and designer accessories at a fraction of the cost.

"Well, it all sounds fascinating," she says.

"It was but I'm really looking forward to getting back to my go-sees and auditions," I say, hoping I can steer the conversation back. "I'm ready to pick up exactly where I left."

Judith is silent. She looks at me and tilts her head to the side. "Brit, you know, a year is a long time . . ." She's telling *me* a year is a long time? Try spending that year away from the one thing you love? "And, well, a lot changes in a year."

Judith has never beat around the bush with me before. She has always treated me like a professional. "What are you trying to say?" I ask.

"I'm just saying that there is the possibility you might not pick up *exactly* where you left off."

Now I am the one who is silent. What does she mean? Of course I plan to pick up where I left off. Why wouldn't I? I wait for Judith to elaborate but she doesn't.

"Look," she continues "why don't we just take this one step at a time. You're back and I'm thrilled to have you back. We'll get you out on some appointments this week, but let's just take this one step at a time." She says that "one step at a time" thing twice and the way she says it the second time makes me feel funny, like I should be worried about something, but then I realize she also mentioned getting me out on some appointments by the end of the week.

All I really need is my shot in front of the camera and I'll be able to show Judith that for Brittany Rush, "one step" will be a giant leap.

CHAPTER 4

Hong Kong was all neon lights and bright colors. The streets circled and crossed over each other in such a way that you could get lost before you were at the end of a block. New York is the exact opposite. The buildings are gray and massive and the city is almost a perfect grid, making it nearly impossible to get confused. Most of the casting offices are located between Fourteenth Street and Twenty-third Street around the Flatiron building, an ornate, turn-of-the-century masterpiece with a triangle shape. It sits at the base of Madison Square Park between Twenty-second and Twenty-third Street. Once I did a social studies report on the building since I walk by it so often.

Judith called only a day after our meeting in her office. My first appointment: Betsy Barnes Casting. I can't actually remember how many spots I've booked through this office. Dozens, maybe even more. When I was a toddler, I booked a major commercial for Toy Box stores that ran every Christmas for about three years. Before I left for stupid Hong Kong, I booked a print ad through Betsy Barnes for an online clothing store. I know every single person who works in the office so when I go through the revolving door to go up to my appointment, I know this audition for a new line of healthy cookies called Organica will be a snap.

Nothing has changed in the lobby. The same ancient security guard with the long, gray beard is reading the paper and still doesn't bother to even look up when someone enters the building. The familiarity of it all makes me smile. I walk past the desk and push the button for the elevator and wait. As I'm waiting, the revolving door spins and a mother and daughter enter.

The mother has a piece of paper in her hand and immediately begins scanning the building directory sign. "Carla," she says to the girl, "let me just find the right floor." The girl, who is maybe a year or so younger than me, just looks around the lobby. She is clearly a newbie. I can spot them a mile away. First of all, anyone who has been around the block knows that Betsy Barnes is on seventeen. Barnes casts a quarter of the spots in town and if you have even been going out for less than a month, you know the only floor that matters in this building is seventeen.

The newbie is cute in a simple sort of way, but she's done everything wrong. First she is wearing too much makeup. I can actually see a frosty-pink color on her lips. Casting agents do not like girls wearing anything too beauty-pageant-circuit. Second, her hair is totally wrong. It has a nice texture but she has bangs that fall in front of her face. Casting agents want to see your face. Duh. Finally her outfit is just . . . wrong. It's an adorable black-and-white houndstooth dress. But you NEVER wear a dress unless the casting office has specifically asked to see you in one—not to mention that you NEVER wear a *print*. Prints interfere with the camera lens and make it look like you are wearing an ant farm.

The mother is still scanning the directory when I say, "Excuse me, are you looking for Betsy Barnes Casting? The Organica spot?"

"Yes, yes," the mother says.

"It's on seventeen," I say as sweetly as possible. I figure this girl isn't even going to come close to getting a callback so there is no harm in helping her.

"Thank you so much. The directory isn't even

alphabetical." I can tell she is relieved. "Is this your first time here too?" she asks.

I almost laugh out loud and tell them that in sixth grade I think I spent more time at Betsy's than I did in Mrs. Jensen's math class, but instead I just say, "Not exactly."

The elevator arrives and all three of us get in. As soon as the doors close the mother starts fussing at the girl. She adjusts her dress, tries to smooth out her hair (Good luck!), and actually applies *more* of that strange frosted-pink lip gloss. I actually feel sorry for the girl. My mom may have kept me hostage in Hong Kong for a year, but when she took me on auditions she never "adjusted" me in the way I see some mothers do. Why do mothers think they know how to be a thirteen-year-old girl better than an actual thirteen-year-old girl?

The elevator arrives on the seventeenth floor and they turn right, following the big arrow on the sign that says CASTING, and I wait for them to get halfway down before I turn left to my secret prep area.

About three years ago I found this quiet spot in the back stairwell where no one ever bothers to go. There is a small bathroom in the waiting room, but I hate competing with a dozen other girls just to get a small sliver of mirror. I put my bag on the ground and search for my mirror. I use a rather large traveling mirror because it is absolutely essential to be camera-ready from the first moment you enter the room.

This entrance is important since it has been over a year since I've seen Betsy or her assistants Julie or Timmy, for that matter. I'm sure they'll want to hear all about Hong Kong. I check my teeth for any runaway pieces of food and hope that Timmy and Julie won't be too disappointed when they find out I can't stay and chat because of my next appointment.

I head out of the stairwell and as soon as I turn down the hall, I see the sign-in table. I almost have to pause to catch my breath.

I walk down the hall and, as I get closer to the table, I realize the person sitting behind it is not Timmy or Julie. I have no idea who it is. Before I can even say hello, the middle-aged woman behind the sign-in desk starts barking orders at me. "First you need to sign in and use your SAG name if you are SAG. If you are not SAG then just write your name and agency and . . ."

Not SAG? What is wrong with this woman? I've been a member of the Screen Actor's Guild since, literally, before I could walk. Seriously, I was paying union dues while I was in diapers. I decide not to let the insult upset me. The woman is probably just some temp filling in for the afternoon. She probably doesn't even know what SAG stands for.

"I've actually been here before," I tell her. She stops her instructions and kind of looks at me funny. "Many times," I say and she still doesn't seem to acknowledge who I am. "Many, many times."

She looks me up and down and says, "Well, sweetie, I've never seen you before and I've been working for Betsy for the last six months. Who's your agent?"

"Judith Lister," I say calmly.

"Oh, you must be Jenny Saunders," she says, looking at her clipboard.

"I'm Brittany Rush," I say slowly and deliberately. I want to tell her that if she ever turned on a TV she might actually know that, but I just sign my name on the sign-in sheet and grab the sides from her.

"Studio two," she says. "It's down the other hall, turn left at—"

"I know where it is," I say, cutting her off as I walk toward the studio.

Before I enter the studio, I look over the sides.

All sides are a bit different. Some just have the script of the commercial on them. These have a full storyboard with grids of boxes where someone from some advertising company has drawn their vision of what should be happening on the screen as the lines are being said.

I read over the sides and quickly see this is what's called a "bite and smile" spot. That means all you have to do is pretend you are about to eat the most delicious thing in the world. Pretend to take a bite and then smile like you won the lottery. Piece of cake. I've done it a thousand times. Usually during the first audition they are too cheap to use the real product so they have some bag of stale potato chips. Although once I did a "bite and smile" for a potato chip commercial and they used Oreos.

Go figure.

I take a breath before I open the door to Studio Two. I know what usually happens when I enter a studio of girls waiting to be seen. It's not pretty. Once at a callback a girl actually left when she saw me enter the room because she knew if I was there she had no chance of booking it. I know it's terrible, but I get sort of a rush when I walk in and everyone knows they are ready for some serious competition.

When I open the door, everyone in the room turns to look at me. But then something strange happens. *They go back to what they were doing.* No one examines what I'm wearing. No one checks to see if my hair is above or below my shoulders this month. No one runs out of the room crying.

Very odd.

I take a seat on one of the folding metal chairs and look around the room, since I don't really have to rehearse any lines. A year ago at my last audition almost every girl was with her mother or some other form of guardian, but now there is more of a mix. Some girls, like me, are on their own, while others are still with someone. Besides that, there's still something else about this group that is both strange and familiar. Then I suddenly see her and not just one of her; *two* of her. Two of the girls at the audition are wearing my Kate. I am furious. Kate is mine. Do they have any idea how long it took me to realize the perfect outfit for each audition? They have copied me down to the exact shade of teal. I feel like ripping the shirts right off their backs.

I should have known this would happen. The year I started parting my hair on the side, suddenly everyone else started parting their hair on the side.

When I replaced my gold heart earrings with small silver hoops, there was suddenly an abundance of small silver hoops.

After about ten minutes another assistant, who must also be new, calls my name and I walk into the studio. Sure, landing at JFK and walking through the front door of our house in Great Neck felt like coming *back* but this, this is coming home.

Studio Two is only the size of a large closet, but to me the cramped quarters, the silver umbrella bouncing light from the tungsten, the tripod with the camera mounted to the base are like a favorite pillow or patch of grass in the backyard. I am finally home.

I peek around the camera looking for Betsy.

"Betsy?" I say, "I'm baaack." The light is shining in my eyes so I can't really see past the camera, but I see a figure move toward me. I expect to see Betsy's flaming red hair but instead I hear a giggle.

"No, no. I'm not Betsy," the voice says in between nervous giggles. "I'm Vicky Chow." A very tiny Asian woman with huge, round glasses comes out from behind the camera. "Do you know Betsy?"

Do I know Betsy? Please. She's only the person who hired the clown for my sixth birthday. Yeah, I know Betsy.

"Where is she?" I ask, hoping she is working in another studio or just in her office.

More giggling and then, "Oh, she's been gone for about six months. She's redoing her house in the Hamptons and she's been spending most of her time out there lately. I've been running things in the meantime." More giggling and then Vicky goes back behind the camera and says, "Okay, we are going to slate first. That means . . ."

I can't take it any more.

"Vicky, I know what a slate is. Just hand me the bag of chips and start rolling. I'll be fine," I say. My anger is impossible to repress any more. Vicky stops giggling, hands me the bag, and the camera starts rolling.

CHAPTER 5

If I weren't worried about making my eyes puffy for my next go-see, I would be walking down the street in tears.

How can so much change in twelve stupid months? It's not my fault my family moved to Hong Kong so my Mom could stop freelancing and become a full-time staff reporter. Why am *I* being punished?

Not a single person in the room knew who I was or even recognized me. I was just one of the names on the list, just one of the girls wearing a teal polo shirt.

As I walk down Fifth Avenue toward my next audition, I suddenly realize something that will snap me out of my foul mood in a matter of seconds. There is a Berger's Burgers on Seventeenth Street. I usually avoid this fast-food chain like a PE class on a hot afternoon, but today I could use a little pick-me-up. As soon as I turn the corner onto Seventeenth Street, the trademark purple and orange lights practically assault my eyes.

Even though it was over three years ago, I remember the day I booked the Berger's Burgers campaign like it was yesterday. Judith was so thrilled she actually bought me my very own pink iPod. Every time a company airs a commercial you are in or runs a print ad with your face, or really any recognizable part of your body, they need to pay you and your agent money. The fact that my face was going to be plastered all over the menus, commercials, print ads, and in-store displays meant *beaucoup* bucks for both me and Judith. After the campaign rolled out I had to stop going to Berger's Burgers as my presence often caused a bit of a commotion. "You're the girl! You're her!" people would call out.

A few times at the Berger's Burgers in Hicksville, a few people actually asked me to sign their burger wrapper. Of course, I obliged. Usually I tend to avoid all the fuss, but at this moment I realize I could use a little fuss.

I open the door and, as I suspected, right on the wall next to the trash can is a picture of me eating a burger on a poster advertising the Berger Bacon Burger. It's a little embarrassing since my hair is in pigtails in the picture and I haven't worn my hair like that for a few years now. I hope no one asks me about the pigtails.

Usually I am recognized before I even make it to the counter to place my order, but today I'm able to make it to the front of the store without too much commotion. I am in the middle of Manhattan so it's not exactly like being in the suburbs. *Here* they're used to seeing famous people. Still, as I look around, I think a few people are making the connection.

At least, I think so.

I linger by the counter next to the poster with my face on it. In this one I'm using one of the big purple napkins to wipe the corners of my mouth since, according to the poster, the burgers are just that juicy. In reality I find them a little dry and tasteless but they don't book you for portraying the truth; they book you for being able to create an illusion.

I stand next to the poster for a few minutes.

Nothing.

Customers walk right past me without even so much as a glance. I even grab a purple napkin from the condiment bar and wipe the corners of my mouth with it. Surely, this will create some sort of response.

Still nothing happens.

In one of the commercials for the campaign I'm in, they show me waiting in line with a fake mom and when it's our turn to order, I go right to the counter and say, "I'll have a Berger's Burgers kids' meal, cause I'm a kid." Then I point to myself with my thumb and everyone around chuckles, and then it cuts to me enjoying my meal at a table with my fake family.

Since standing next to the poster does not seem to be getting any response, I get in line with the other customers at the counter as a last-ditch effort. When it's my turn to order, a girl only a few years older than me is standing behind the counter.

She sighs audibly before rolling her eyes and saying. "Berger's Burgers can't be beat. Can I take your order?"

I quickly look around to make sure there are at least a few people within earshot and say, "I'll have a kids' meal, cause I'm a kid." I don't use my thumb to point to myself since I figure that would be pushing it a little too much.

The girl behind the counter doesn't immediately punch in the order. Instead she just looks at me and squints her eyes.

This is it.

She knows me.

"Wait a second," she says. Yep. She definitely knows me. I hope I don't have to sign too many autographs. I don't want to be late for my next go-see. She keeps looking at me and says, "You have to be ten or under to order a kids' meal. You're too old."

I look at the column of kids' meals stacked behind her with *my* smiling face repeating like a row of dominoes moments before the chain reaction. I reach my arm across the counter, point at the boxes, and shout. "That's me! I'm ON THE BOX!"

Now people are looking. Granted no one recognizes me still, but the shouting has certainly caused some people to look in my direction. The girl behind the counter looks at the boxes and then at me and shrugs. "Guess it was a while ago. You want something different?"

"Yes," I say and turn on my heel.

I walk out the store and back to the sidewalk where the busy street immediately renders me invisible. This time I can't stop the tears from running down my face. I definitely want something different. I just have to figure out how to get it.

CHAPTER 6

Since coming back home, I have learned there is no limit to the number of things that have forgotten me. Even the couch in our family room has betrayed me. Before I left, my favorite spot to watch TV was lying on the couch with my head propped up on one arm and my feet perfectly elevated by the opposite arm. Now when I am on the couch my heels hang over one end while the other end forces my back into an uncomfortable arch.

Still, it is impossible for me to do anything else but be supine on the couch and mindlessly flip through the channels while simultaneously stuffing my face with some low-carb veggie chips. Usually I flip around the channels looking for the commercials, but today I purposefully make sure that I flip the channel before a commercial even has a *chance* to begin.

When my mother announced we were moving last year, I thought that was the worst day of my life. Now I realize that day was just the first drop in the bucket that is the utter disaster called my life at this very moment.

I thought I'd simply lose a year of bookings. Sure that would be terrible, but I figured once I got back home I would just pick up where I left off. Two auditions today and not one person even acknowledged who I am. I must have at least looked familiar to some of the other girls or at least some of the people in the casting office. Both auditions were total disasters. No one froze up when they saw me or cried because I had returned. Not a single tantrum at either of my go-sees.

Depressing.

I guess Judith was trying to warn me about this possibility. But when someone presses the pause button on your life for an entire year, the second they release it you can't help but want to pick up where you left off.

The program on the TV cuts to a commercial break and instead of racing to change the channel I just squeeze the remote with my hand and shut the stupid thing off. I stare up at the ceiling, unable to believe that this is my life. Washed up at thirteen.

I hear the back door open and my mom and Christine coming back from a trip to the grocery store. They'd asked me if I wanted to go with them but I was just too depressed to walk down those aisles of perfectly placed boxes and cans and see someone else's face staring out at me. There was a time I couldn't go to the grocery store without thinking of it like a hall of mirrors. Now I'd be lucky if they let me bag groceries.

I know I should go help put away the groceries but instead I stay immobile. "Brittany," my mother says, walking into the family room. "I hope you are not planning to lie on the couch watching TV all summer."

I don't even turn my head to look at her. I just say, "Mom, the TV isn't even on." I'd roll my eyes but she can't even see me from where she is standing.

"That's not the point. It's summer and the weather is beautiful. Don't you want to go to the pool club or outside and play?"

Outside and play? How old does she think I am? I just spent the better part of the morning in the city attending a variety of auditions on my own. Clearly I am above the age where I would spend my time playing. Instead of fighting her on this, I just say, "No."

"I'm sure you could tag along with Christine at soccer camp. They have a pool there and lots of other kids. Doesn't that sound fun?"

Hearing her name and soccer camp mentioned, Christine bounces into the room and plops herself down in the chair next to the couch, grabbing the remote. She turns on the TV and starts flipping channels.

"No," I shout back to my mother. When will my mother understand that just because Christine and I are sisters does not mean we like the same things.

"Mom," Christine says while still looking at the television, "Brit doesn't want to tag along with her big sister." Then she looks at me and says, "But the pool is totally cool and they just installed this new diving board."

I give her a look as if to say, *I thought you were on my side*, and she understands my facial expression exactly. She turns back to the TV and says, "I'm just saying is all."

My mother is undaunted by Christine's statement. "Well, I'm just saying that you need something to do this summer . . ."

I tune out my mother, look at my watch and realize there is almost no chance of getting a callback for anything I auditioned for. Usually I get a call from my agent before six o'clock and it's already 6:15. Two auditions today and not one stinking call-back. I can't remember that ever happening before. I don't book *everything* I go out for, but not getting a callback after two auditions? Not even a nibble? I pull the cushion off the back of the couch and pull it over my face.

"Brittany Marie! Do not hide under that cushion while I am in the middle of talking to you."

I realize I have totally zoned my mother out and, considering I may spend the summer stuck at home, I better make sure I am not grounded on top of it. "Sorry, Mom. What were you saying?"

"I was telling you about this," she says and hands me a piece of blue paper. "They were handing out flyers downtown today in front of the market." I sit up from the couch and take the flyer from her. SUMMER ART CLASSES it says in bold, hand-designed letters across the top. "It looks like they have classes for kids your age. Why don't you sign up? You were really into your art classes in Hong Kong. You didn't go anywhere without your sketchbook."

I look at my watch. 6:22. I realize that there really isn't going to be much to do this summer anyway.

Christine is going to be in soccer camp pretty much every day all day so I might as well have something to do if I am not going to be going out on go-sees. I look at the flyer and say, "Maybe I'll go downtown and register."

I drag myself off the couch and head out of the family room and up the stairs. Before I can make it to the second floor I hear the sound of my muffled ring tone. I pat my pocket and realize I must have left my cell phone downstairs and IT'S RINGING! I fly back down the stairs and, almost knocking over my mother, leap to the couch in the family room. I don't see my cell phone but I can hear it ringing. I shove my hand beneath the cushions and fish for the dang thing, finally grabbing it before it stops ringing. I don't even look at the caller ID.

"Hello," I say.

"Hey Brit. I have a callback for you for the Shane's Supermarket spot."

YES! YES! YES! I'm back. I knew it. I knew it was impossible for me to go on two auditions and not get at least one callback. I'm not ready to reveal my desperation to Judith so I just say, "Just the one? Well, let me get something to write everything down with . . ." I hold my finger over the mouthpiece and jump up and down, shrieking with joy. I grab a pencil from the desk and take the flyer for art classes out of my pocket, rip it in half, and start writing on the back of it. Who needs art classes when I am about to make my big comeback?

CHAPTER 7

A callback. I knew it.

Callbacks are where I really shine. Auditions are like shopping at a huge swap meet. Sometimes it's hard to stand out when you are surrounded by so much cheap merchandise. A callback is more like shopping in a boutique. Only a few items to choose from, but only the best quality.

As I walk down Broadway toward Mel Bethany Casting on Twenty-second Street, I repeat my lines over and over. The commercial has two scenes. The first scene shows a girl, that would be me, shopping with her mother. The girl is planning on making dinner for the family on her own for the first time and she is shopping with her mother for the ingredients. At one point I say, "Relax, Mom, I'll take care of dinner."

The second scene takes place around a dining room table. I bring out the dinner, everyone enjoys it in typical commercial fashion, and at the end my mom compliments me and I say, "Thanks, but you're doing the dishes." The whole family laughs and blah, blah, blah.

My agent once told me that the key to booking at a callback is to give the director choices. "Show them you can do anything," Judith told me, so I always make sure I have a bunch of ways to say my lines. Like on the first take I might say, "Relax, Mom, I'll take care of dinner," like I'm really looking forward to making dinner. On the second take I might say it like I just came up with the idea on the spot. The third might be like I'm a little worried about being in charge of a new responsibility. I rehearse each line so that they just roll off my tongue.

By the time I am actually in front of the building, I feel a bit nervous. The callback is just one step away from a booking. I know if I can just book this spot I'll be able to recover my momentum. I can't get nervous. Nerves will freeze me up and make me seem about as awkward on camera as a rack of ribs at a vegetarian restaurant. I try to calm down and take a deep breath in and out before taking the elevator up.

Mel Bethany Casting has two glass doors that open in to the waiting room. Upon getting out of the elevator, I walk past the doors as if I am going to any other office—like the dentist. This gives me just enough time to survey the competition. Out of the corner of my eye I can spot at least four other girls and even more fake moms. That's a good sign. When there are fewer called back for your type it means they are closer to making a decision. The only other detail I could glean is that all the girls have long hair like mine. That's also good. Sometimes they bring in someone with a totally different look, like a sassy, short haircut, and the director finds that refreshing. I consider doing another drive by but realize that it would be conspicuous, and the last thing I want is for any of the other girls to think I am desperate.

I walk through the glass doors. The others turn and look at me, but they would look at anyone who came through the door. Tensions run high at a call-back since everyone knows the only thing standing between them and booking is you—the person in the room who books the spot.

I go to grab my size card off the desk and staring back at me I see the picture that was taken of me the other day at the audition. I am, of course, wearing the same exact outfit. I don't know if this is tradition or strategy, but everyone I know who books wears the same thing to the audition and then the callback. Judith says, "If it worked at the audition, it will work again."

I see that there are a few cards that have not yet been picked up, which means that there are more girls for the callback than I originally thought. I take my card and the woman behind the desk says, "We are going by call time, not arrival. There are copies of the sides here." She points to a pile of papers in front of her. I take one even though I have every millisecond of the spot memorized already. The fact that we are going by call time rather than arrival means that I might go in ahead of a lot of the girls who got here before me. I look at my watch and see that my call time is pretty close. I take a chair away from everyone else to examine the situation.

It's the usual collection of girls like me. Each is on her own or with some relative or even their real mom. Scattered about are a smattering of fake moms also preparing for the audition. The real moms always look older, tired, and stressed out. Before my mom started letting me go out on appointments on my own, she always fit in well with the real moms since she is older, often tired, and *always* stressed out. The fake moms are younger, attractive, and thin. I recognize a few of them and even think there is one I booked a spot with before I left. I could go over and socialize but I want to stay focused on the task at hand.

The studio door pops open and a girl and fake mom walk out. Everyone looks quickly at them and then a few of the pros look at their watches. They want to know how long they were in the studio. Usually longer is better. When they keep you in there it means they are seriously considering you. When they don't want you, they know pretty quickly.

"Alexa Ferrin and Brittany Rush," a girl with a clipboard announces while standing in the doorway to the studio. I take a deep breath and quickly once-over the woman going in to be my fake mom for the next six minutes. I grab my backpack, smile at Alexa, and we walk into the studio together.

Most casting offices are small closet-like spaces, but Mel's shop has large, spacious studios where the client and director sit on overstuffed couches at the back of the room while they whisper about the people in front of the camera.

"Hi, Alexa and Brittany. I'm Mike Michaels, the

director of this little spot," says a man with overly manicured facial hair and a baseball cap that is most likely covering up a middle-aged bald spot. He gets up from the couch where a bunch of other business types are sitting. Most likely they are the clients, the people who own whatever it is the commercial is for, and the creatives, the people who wrote, designed, and created the commercial about to be shot. "Now what we are going for here is really big energy, but really big natural that is also very small."

I look over at Alexa. She looks confused. I, on the other hand, smile broadly and say, "Great. I got it." The truth is, I too have no idea what a very small big natural is but I'm used to directors speaking a foreign language. Even if what he said made total sense and I executed it exactly, there is still no guarantee I'll book the spot. I learned years ago the key to pleasing a director is to make him feel like you understand even when you don't.

Alexa and I move in front of the camera and slate by saying our names and agencies. The guy behind the camera yells, "Hands!" which means we need to show the front and the back of our hands in front of our faces before we start. This usually means the commercial involves some sort of close-up that features your hands. They want to make sure that you aren't missing any fingernails I guess.

The person behind the camera gives us a count-down and we run through the scene. I think I do pretty well on the first take. Not my best, but certainly better than most of the other girls in the waiting area will probably do. Alexa and I stand in silence in front of the camera and wait.

On the couch, Mike is whispering with the clients and the creatives. It's impossible to hear what they are whispering but I imagine Mike is telling them about what he will be "going for" on the next take. Alexa turns to me and smiles, which I think is very nice. I smile back at her and wonder if she recognizes me. Mike breaks the huddle and says, "Thank you both," and then goes back to the couch huddle.

Alexa goes toward the door but I don't. I just stand there for a few seconds. *Thank you?* Did I just hear the words "thank you"? Seriously? After one take I am getting shown the door? I didn't even get to do any of the choices I had prepared. Thank you? Does this guy even know who I am?

Be professional, I tell myself. It's a small commercial world and if I have a tantrum it means Mike Michaels will never hire me for a future spot. I step off my mark and walk out the door behind Alexa.

My plan is to walk out of the studio and keep going until I am on the other side of the glass doors and out of the building so I can have my tantrum on the street. But before I can make my way out, I hear a very familiar sound that stops me dead in my tracks.

CHAPTER 8

I know this sound. It's the sound of hopes dashing on rocky shores. It's like a school lunch tray slipping out of your hands in the middle of the cafeteria, the moment before the tray hits the floor. Every single girl in the waiting area snaps her head toward the door and after seeing who has entered, looks down in despair. I am not unfamiliar with the scenario; I'm just used to being the one who provokes it.

I look carefully at the girl who has just entered and it takes me only a second to realize that it's Phoebe Marks.

I almost laugh out loud.

I've known Phoebe since I was a little girl and there is no way she is the current It Girl. I move my head to look behind her to see if someone more dynamic and interesting is there. There isn't. It's just

Phoebe. The same girl who went on audition after audition never booking the spots I was cast in. The same girl who would get so nervous at auditions that she would actually forget her lines, even when her lines consisted of one single syllable like "yes."

"O! M! G! You're back!" Phoebe shrieks and runs over to me, placing me in a hug so tight that pro wrestlers would be envious. "Why didn't you call me and let me know you were back? You know, you never gave me your e-mail so we could connect while you were gone? I'm so glad you are back!"

It takes me a second but I quickly remember that Phoebe was under the strange delusion that we were friends. We weren't. Not even close. I would say that, at best, we were rivals, but since she almost never booked a spot over me, we weren't really rivals either. I remember our parents became friendly but that was the extent of it. Phoebe and I were basically strangers who happened to be at the same place at the same time a lot, but Phoebe always thought we were great friends.

It all comes back to me suddenly. I was even invited to a sleepover at her house since we live close to each other, and I considered going until I booked a spot that we were both up for. I remember accepting the invitation because a lot of commercials seemed to be set at sleepovers and since I had never actually been to one, I thought attending Phoebe's would be good research. Accepting the invitation to Phoebe's had nothing to do with being friends with her. That idea never even crossed my mind. I've just always had a deep interest in what girls my age do since I so often play one on TV.

The door to the studio swings open and then I hear Mike Michaels say, "Phoebe, you're here," with so much enthusiasm that it tops Phoebe's shriek from a few moments ago.

Phoebe looks over my shoulder, sees Mike and says, "Just a minute, Mike. I'm just saying hello to a good friend I haven't seen in a while." That statement is pretty ripe for analysis since the only thing mildly accurate is the fact that we haven't seen each other in a long time. Regardless, the real shocker here is that she just told the director, the guy we are all here trying to impress, to hold on. This girl has a screw loose.

I'm about to fall over from shock when I hear Mike say, "Sure, no problem, Phoebe. We will take you whenever you're ready." Hold the phone. Hold the *bleeping* phone because I just heard the director of the spot say that they would basically work around Phoebe.

Phoebe Marks? Forgetful Phoebe?

Mike looks down at his call sheet and yells out, "I'll see Faith Willis and Nancy Dowd." A daughter and mother hopeful stand up and get ready to go in the studio.

"We should hang out at the pool or something now that you are back," Phoebe says, and then sees that she is disrupting the entire callback. "Mike," she says, "I'm ready now if you are." The freshly called mother and daughter sit back down and Phoebe waltzes past the other girls and into the studio. She wiggles her fingers in a childish wave good-bye and the door closes behind her. I look at the girls still waiting to go in. Most of them just stare at the door Phoebe went through. They are imagining the lovefest that is going on in the studio, as Phoebe is one step closer to booking the spot. As soon as the door shuts, these girls realize that any chance they had of booking the spot has disappeared. For a second I feel sorry for them until I realize I am one of them.

CHAPTER 9

My family thinks Im crazy. They cannot understand why in the world I would ever want to spend my time on commercials when I could have a perfectly normal summer like Christine and every other kid in Great Neck, Long Island, going to the mall or hanging at our swim club.

Being in a commercial is like being famous for thirty seconds. All of a sudden the world stops and everything is focused on you and the new soda you are drinking or ice cream you are tasting. I was hooked from the very start and my parents never once tried to stop me.

When I was younger, my mom was a freelance writer so she had time to take me on auditions, and we would both just stare in disbelief at the pushy "stage mothers" who seemed to dominate the waiting rooms.

My mother has always been the exact opposite of a stage mother. In the beginning, whenever I booked something she would ask, "Are you sure you want to do this? I can just call them back and tell them you would rather go play outside." Or something equally ridiculous. My mom quickly learned that I would much rather pretend to play outside on the set of a commercial than *actually* play outside.

I look at the calendar in the kitchen with Christine's soccer dates on it and realize that it has been six days since I have had to go into the city for an audition or a callback. I stare at my bowl of cereal, moving my spoon around the corn flakes.

My dad seems to sense that I am depressed and tries to say something to cheer me up. "Looks like it's going to be near one hundred degrees today, Brit. Bet you sure are glad you don't have to go into the city. Those sidewalks are going to feel like they are on fire."

I don't say anything. I just keep pushing the corn flakes around in my bowl and wondering when my phone will ring again. Probably everyone can tell I am majorly depressed. They look at one another and crunch their eyebrows together as if to say, *I am worried Brit is majorly depressed.*

Even Christine, who usually just bounces along with the happiness of her own life, can see that something is wrong with me. "Hey," she says, "you could hang out at the pool while I am at soccer camp. It's a really great pool and lots of kids hang out there."

I do wish Christine would stop trying to sell me on the pool. The last thing my hair needs is to be soaking in some chlorine-filled public pool, while a bunch of kids waste my time talking about the latest reality show reject.

"I could meet you when I'm done, and we could play Marco Polo like when we were little," she adds. For a second I remember the summers when we were kids and we would both spend hours at the pool just playing and hanging out. I was still going out on auditions back then, but somehow I also managed to just be a kid. Commercials were part of my life, but now that I am older I realize they are *more* than just a part of my life.

"Look, I'm fine," I say. The last thing I want is for my family worrying about me. "I just need Judith to call me with a go-see. I'm sure she'll call soon." Of course, I am not sure of this at all, but I figure if I say it out loud maybe it will convince my family.

"You know, Brit, if you are dead-set on getting

in touch with Judith," my dad says, "I have to meet a client in the city today not too far from her office. I could drive you in." Usually I am only allowed to go to the city when I have an appointment. Some kids would die just to be allowed to take the train in to shop or hang out. Personally, if I don't have an appointment, I don't see the need to be there.

"Dad, I don't have anything scheduled for today," I tell him, reminding myself of the terrible slump I am in.

"I know," he says. "I just thought that maybe you would want to come in with me, and maybe you could stop by and see Judith face-to-face."

I drop my spoon in my soggy bowl of corn flakes. "Dad, that's a great idea," I say and run upstairs to get ready and change. Of course. Seeing Judith face-to-face is just the thing I need to get me over this slump.

CHAPTER 10

On the way into the city I call Judith to let her know I'm coming. I've stopped by unannounced before so it shouldn't be an issue—but still, I want to let her know. I dial the familiar number as my dad fights the traffic on the Long Island Expressway. After the second ring I hear Judith's assistant, Peggy, on the voice mail. "Hello, you have reached the voice mail of Judith Lister of the A-Lister Agency. We are unable to take your call at the moment. Please leave a message." Peggy's Brooklyn accent is strangely comforting in this moment.

At the tone I decide to leave a short message. "Hi, everyone. It's Brittany. I just wanted to let you know that I am coming into the city with my dad and I thought I would stop in. See you soon. Bye."

I hang up and my dad pats my leg with his hand. "See," he says, "I can tell you are feeling better already." I smile for the first time in what seems like days, because he's right, I actually do feel better. I just need some guidance from Judith.

When I walk into the agency's office, Peggy greets me with a hug and a big smile. This immediately makes me feel better. She buzzes Judith to let her know I'm here and I am quickly ushered into Judith's office. Everyone at A-Lister treats me like royalty and it's nice to be treated special for a change.

Judith finishes a phone call while I sit in the chair across from her desk. She hangs up, puts back on the clip earring she had taken off to talk on the phone, and says, "So, to what do I owe the pleasure of this visit?"

I pause before answering. The truth is that before I left, my mother was really in charge of working out all of the business stuff with Judith and people in the office. Sure, I was involved but I was only a kid for the most part, just ten or eleven. Now, I'm actually a teenager. My mother doesn't accompany me on every audition and I'm responsible for getting to my appointments on time by myself, like all the other girls my age. I'm suddenly realizing this as I am sitting across from Judith. I don't want to sound like a kid and whine about how I am not going out as much as I used to. The last thing I want to do is become one of those problem clients who constantly complain and quickly get dropped from the agency's roster. Then I remember a phrase I hear my dad use whenever he is on the phone for business and I decide to try it out.

"Well, I just thought I would touch base with you . . . about my career," I say. I like the way the words just roll off my tongue. It sounds very professional.

"Oh, I see," Judith says. She then presses the button on the intercom to the reception area and says, "Peggy, hold my calls while I am in with Brittany." For a second it feels like I am about to be voted off the island, but then Judith gives me a big, understanding smile. "Things have been a little slow, I know."

"I'm not complaining," I say quickly. "I just want to know how I can do a better job."

"Brittany, you are doing a great job. You just had that callback the other day."

"I know, but . . ."

"But it was just one callback," Judith says, resting her head on her hand and looking at me sympathetically.

"Exactly," I say. "It's just that before I left . . ."

"I know, Brit. But we really have to take things one step at a time."

61

Here she goes with that "one step" stuff again. I wish I understood what she meant by that. Then she adds, "Things *have* changed a lot . . ."

"I know," I say. This must be what she means. I try to keep up on the industry news as much as possible. Even when I was in Hong Kong, I went online to read about the industry. "More castings are moving to L.A. and being shot in cheaper locations, like Canada and South America. But online advertising is giving everything a major boost even though it changes the industry."

"Brittany, I'm not talking about how the industry has changed, I'm talking about you."

I can actually feel my eyelids moving a little farther back from my eyes and the lower part of my mouth descending. Is she about to tell me that I am so different from when I left that I have zero chance of ever booking again? I thought I was coming in for a pep talk, not to be let go. I finally find the courage to respond, "Me? You mean, I've changed too much?"

"No, not at all," Judith says as she gets up from her desk and walks around to where I am sitting.

Phew. I knew it. I knew it couldn't be me. I mean, I made sure that I wore my hair the same way I did before I left and delivered my lines the same way, and

I even tried to wear the same audition clothes. It's not me. I haven't changed.

"I mean, you haven't changed *enough*."

"Excuse me?" I ask. What *is* Judith talking about?

She grabs her purse off her desk and opens her door. "Peggy, I'm taking my favorite client out for a smoothie and a chat. I'll be back when I'm back. C'mon Brit." She waves her hand toward me and I follow her out of the office.

"Two large blueberry-mango summer blockbuster smoothies," Judith says to the guy behind the counter before turning to me and saying, "I have been obsessed with these things since this place opened a few months ago. They are amazing."

The Pink Doodle Café looks brand new. Instead of chairs, there are white, molded couches that seem to grow out of the walls and floor, and the lighting feels more like an art gallery than a café. It definitely has a cool vibe, but I am too distracted by worrying about what Judith is going to say to really appreciate any of the atmosphere.

We grab our drinks and sit on one of the empty couches. Judith starts sipping hers and moans, "Aren't these the most divine things you have ever tasted?

Sometimes I just need to get out of the office and clear my head. It helps me take a fresh look at whatever I am working on."

I begin to feel like we're starting the conversation Judith really wants to have. If she is going to drop me, I should be mature. I should just accept it. I should not cry. I will not cry. There will be no crying. "Judith," I begin, trying to sound as calm as possible, "are you going to drop me from the agency?"

"What?" Judith says. "Don't even say that. That's ridiculous."

"Then what did you mean when you said I haven't changed enough?" I ask.

"You are still adorable and better with copy than any person I have ever met. You just naturally know how to read the lines."

"Thanks," I say. I am so desperate for a compliment that I am not about to let one pass unnoticed.

"Right before you left you had just turned twelve and had spent a year going out as an eleven year old booking so much there weren't enough hours in the day to fit it all in, but now, you have just turned thirteen and things are different."

Well you didn't need to buy me a blueberry-mango smoothie to tell me that. I KNOW things are different. I make sure to keep my attitude in check. "I know things are different, Judith. But how do I make things go back to the way they were? That's what I want to know. That's why I came to see you today."

"But Brittany, honey, that's just it. You can't make things go back to the way they were. Things have to be the way they are. You can only move forward in this business. Look, no one your age knows this business better than you. Even when you were a toddler you were able to figure out the exact time to gurgle to catch the director's attention. I never saw anything like it. The thing is, gurgling doesn't work anymore and you just need to find out what does."

I sit in silence and press my lips around the straw of my smoothie. "But Judith, how am I supposed to do that?" I ask, hoping she will have an easy answer.

"I don't know exactly, but if anyone can figure it out, Brittany, it's you."

CHAPTER 11

The next week I have two auditions scheduled. One is for a big-box store and one is for an amusement park. It's an average week in terms of the numbers of auditions but I'm not really concerned about booking either of these. I've decided to use this week as time to re-evaluate what's going on. Judith said I had to figure out what works again. I can do that. I know I can do that. When I was a kid, I would just watch the other kids and do what they did. That's how I figured it out at first. I would just take the time to look around and observe.

Even though my call time is at 11:05 a.m. for the big-box store spot at Double Doors Casting, I take the early train in with my mom so I can get to the office about an hour before. Double Doors is one of a handful of casting offices that uses a suite of studios called Actor's Space. There are about a dozen casting offices on one open floor and they share the same hallway waiting area, which means there is always a ton of people around. Mostly there are adults auditioning for films, TV pilots, even Broadway shows. It sounds glamorous, and in some ways it is, but mostly it's just strange to see adults emoting to a blank wall, rehearsing their lines, or vocalizing in a stairwell.

The elevator doors open and, while most casting offices are somewhat calm as people quietly wait to go in, there is actual mayhem at Actor's Space. People are rehearsing lines, singing, and even practicing short dance combinations. There are senior citizens, adults, kids, and even infants auditioning for everything from the newest independent film to small Web-series productions. In front of the elevator is a huge chalkboard on an easel that someone updates each day. Each studio is assigned a letter of the alphabet and this board explains which studio has what audition. I see that Double Doors Casting is in Studio H today. I also notice that they are casting something for Christine's favorite TV show in Studio B, and for a second I consider scoping out the area to see if I can catch a glimpse of any of the cute boys who always seem to be at those auditions. But instead I realize I need to focus.

Studio H is around the back of the building, which is perfect since it means I can grab one of the chairs near the back entrance without being noticed by anyone coming in. I sign in, take a copy of the sides, and look at them quickly. Yes, I am here to observe but I can't blow off the audition. If you really blow a go-see, they stop asking you back. This audition just shows a mom driving with her daughter in the passenger seat. The camera pans out to reveal that the back seat is full of big sacks of money. Who knows what this means or how this is going to make people want to shop at the big-box store in the commercial? I learned to stop trying to figure these things out a long time ago.

I am the only person my age in the waiting area, which means there is a back up of moms at the moment. I'm sure, later in the day, everything will reverse and there will be a whole waiting area of daughters and only a few moms. I figure there is not much to observe here since it will be decades before I start going out for the mom roles. I take a seat in the back and decide to start preparing for my audition.

How should one react when there are sacks of money in the backseat of their car? Should I be surprised, like, *Hey, how did that money get back there?* Should I be happy, like, *I'm so glad we've got all that money back there?* Or should I just be nonchalant, like, *Oh this? We always have big sacks of money in the backseat of our car.* I try to come up with facial expressions for all three. I'm actually working on my pretend surprise look when it is suddenly replaced by a look of actual surprise at the sight of Phoebe Marks signing in to the audition. She has her back turned to me so I take this opportunity to grab my bag and run to the bathroom. I am not going to be ambushed by her again. This time I am going to be prepared.

In the bathroom I decide that the best defense is a good offense. When I come out I am the one who is going to be all sparkles and sunshine. I'll be delighted to see my old friend. Phoebe barely had anyone to talk to before. I remember her sitting by herself while casting directors would fawn over me. She used to come on auditions with her mother and spend the time waiting with a coloring book. Yes, she actually brought a coloring book to auditions. Poor thing is probably sitting out there right now trying to choose between burnt sienna and fire-engine red for the clown's nose.

I laugh to myself thinking of how foolish I was for being threatened by Forgetful Phoebe. She is just a kid doing this to kill some time between student council and her social studies homework. She's not serious about commercial work like I am. I don't know why I would ever feel threatened by her. I have years of experience on her. I'm known in the business as a booker and that counts for something. It counts for a lot.

I walk out of the bathroom with the most genuine fake smile I can muster and prepare myself to greet Phoebe. When I turn the corner to Studio H, I expect to see Phoebe sitting by herself or perhaps with her coloring book, but instead she is surrounded by a bunch of fake moms who seem to be competing for her attention. How can that be? My genuine fake smile turns into an authentic grimace.

I turn around to go hide in the back until my name is called to go in, but eagle-eyed Phoebe spots me and shouts my name. "Brittany!" I freeze. I could keep walking away, pretending I don't hear her braying voice, but there are car alarms quieter than Phoebe. I would have to be headless to have not heard her.

I turn and pretend I didn't see her. "Oh, Phoebe, I didn't see you," I say. The fake moms surrounding Phoebe look at me suspiciously. I'm not too surprised. Once you book a spot with someone and they play your parent, the truth is, they start to act like your parent.

"Do you know Lisa R.? And Lisa K.?" Phoebe

asks. While both of the women look familiar, I can't say that I actually know either of them so I shake my head. Phoebe takes this as a cue for her introductions. "Well Lisa R. and I booked a spot for a car loan company a few months ago and Lisa K. plays my mom in all of those Pizza Fantastic commercials."

What is going on here? Phoebe Marks actually booking spots? Sure it was a novelty to see her at callbacks now and then. I figured someone would occasionally take pity on her, but to find out that she has actually been booking all of these spots is almost more than I can handle. I try to catch a glimpse of her hands to see if she has been writing the copy on her palms.

"Oh, and did you see, Phoebe?" Lisa K. asks. "They started running the Pizza Fantastic spots where we are all on the boat. They are so cute."

"I've seen those," Lisa R. says. "I think I saw that spot a few times last night on TV. You were both great. They are so funny!"

The door to the studio swings open. "Lisa Ruchlin and Brittany Rush," the assistant casting director says to the crowd waiting.

"Oh darn, Phoebe. I was hoping we would be paired up. I don't even know if this other girl is here."

"She's standing right in front of you," I say. "I'm Brittany."

Lisa laughs heartily to cover her faux pas. "Of course, I'm so sorry," she says and we walk into the studio.

More and more I am beginning to think I am invisible.

We walk in front of the cameras and slate by saying our name and agency. Lisa is with Buckingham Associates, which is a major agency, so even though she appears to have the intelligence of a paper clip, she must be good at what she does. Buckingham does not represent the unbookable.

We run through the scene a few times. I do surprise, delight, and nonchalance with equal skill, and Lisa also has a different expression for each take. This is not her first day at the rodeo.

I let Lisa walk out before me since I am desperate to avoid interacting with Phoebe yet again. I scan the waiting area quickly to make sure Phoebe is not ready to leap at me with another one of her death-grip hugs. Luckily, she is sitting off to the back with her head buried deeply in the sides.

First, I'm surprised to see Phoebe preparing at all.

Second, she is sitting next to some boy and they

are going over the sides together. Now THAT is really strange. Did Phoebe snag some boy from some other audition to help her with the spot? Did she bring her boyfriend to the audition?

Third, the boy is cute with a capital K! He has tousled, sandy-brown hair that falls in front of his face and a wide open smile that is almost a grin. If I weren't so worried about Phoebe spotting me, I would stay and get a closer look since he is definitely as cute as she is annoying. Instead, I dash down the hall, avoiding Phoebe, and head toward my next audition. But I can't help wondering, *Who* is *that boy?*

CHAPTER 12

My second audition is at Betsy Barnes Casting and is for an amusement park. Barnes is only a few blocks away from Double Doors so I am able to get to the audition way ahead of my scheduled appointment to do some useful observation. The elevator doors open and I hit the jackpot. There are girls everywhere. It's like they're giving away free lip gloss. There are already a whole bunch of kids my age sitting and standing around the waiting area. I walk by the sign-in and grab a copy of the sides before heading to a chair near the back where I can sit unnoticed.

Before I begin my observation, I decide to look through the sides to see how much time I will need to spend preparing. This is one of those spots that uses a storyboard instead of just a script for the audition. The storyboard shows pictures of a girl and a boy with a bunch of their friends riding rides and playing games at the park. In the first few squares, the girl is with all of her girl friends and the boy is with all of his guy friends. Then the boy and the girl get stuck in the same car of some ride, and then they are seen holding hands walking around the park. Whoa!

I have been on hundreds of auditions since before I could walk. I have played an endless number of sisters, daughters, students, and best friends. I even played the role of a baby acorn, but I have never had to hold hands with a boy for an audition or pretend to be his girlfriend. Usually I worry about whether I'll get paired up with a mother who will totally blow the audition and make me look bad, or a dad who's creepy. Now I have to worry about whether or not my hand sweats too much.

I go back to my chair away from the studio that allows me to see all of the action but stay above the fray. The first thing I notice is that the boys and the girls are sitting in different areas, which is weird. I don't remember that happening at auditions before I left. The kids on set and at auditions always hung out together and only distanced themselves from the adults. Since it is unlikely that I will ever have to compete against any of the boys, I focus my attention on the girls and am grateful for this divide since it makes my job easier.

The first thing I notice is that some of the girls are a bit older than me, maybe fourteen or even older. I recognize one of the girls from a commercial for a face moisturizer for teens. She definitely seems older. She is a little taller than the other girls, who are about my height. She's wearing jeans and a bright blue shirt with a scoop neck.

Judith told me to pay attention to what the other girls were doing, how they looked, what they wore, or even how they behaved at the auditions. I take out my sketchbook in order to jot down a few notes. I start to write down a description of each girl's outfit, but after a few seconds I realize my descriptions are lame. I have "blue, pretty shirt" and "other blue shirt, not as pretty." When I get home to study these, I'll be more confused than when I began. I switch from a blue ballpoint pen to a pencil with a sharp point and long edge. Instead of writing notes to keep track of what is going on, I decide to create some sketches as a way of observing the situation.

The one, and perhaps only, good thing that happened to me in Hong Kong was Mrs. Bayer's art class. Before her class I had never even picked up a sketchpad and pencil. But by the end of her class, I was constantly walking around with a sketchbook and drawing whatever I happened to see. In Hong Kong there was so much to draw. Around every corner was a new vista and something I had never seen before. Mrs. Bayer thought my sketches were fantastic and often put them on the bulletin board for everyone to see. I enjoyed that. Since coming back home, I realized I have carried my sketchbook around but I haven't actually drawn anything.

I turn the page of my sketchbook so I can start with a perfectly clean page. My pencil makes contact with the rough paper and, instantly, I am translating what is in front of my eyes to the page. I start working on the blue, pretty shirt and, quickly, what was a generic verbal description becomes a collection of lines and shadows.

After drawing the blue shirts and everything else I can observe, from haircuts to fingernail length, I start drawing the rest of the studio just for fun. Within ten minutes I have changed a few of the blank pages of my sketchbook into actual drawings. They look pretty good, although I still need to work on my perspective. The line that I have drawn to delineate the part of the room where the wall meets the ceiling is a bit too shallow. I should have made it steeper to give the drawing more of a sense of depth.

I start rummaging around in my bag for a suitable eraser, leaving the drawing on my lap, when I hear a voice say, "Hey, your use of shading is amazing but, ugh, your perspective needs work."

Rude.

I quickly look up from my bag to see who could be making such a rude comment and it's The Boy. The super cute boy who was with Phoebe outside the last audition. The boy with the floppy hair and the grin. Except now I can't even register his physical appearance; all I can do is scour at him. How dare he be so critical of my drawing? I immediately turn the page in my sketchbook so only a blank page is showing.

"Thank you," I say as sarcastically as possible and sneer at The Boy. There is no level of cuteness that will excuse this level of rudeness.

"Oh, no problem," he says, waving his hand in front of him. It's obvious that my attempt to scorn him has gone unnoticed. He grabs a pencil out of his back pocket and then actually takes my sketchbook out of my hand. MY sketchbook. He starts drawing on the blank page. "See," he says, as if this is a totally sane thing to do. "When you work with perspective, you need to focus on the vanishing point like this." He draws a few simple lines on the paper and they magically turn into a real space. For a moment I'm paying attention to his drawing and what he is saying since he actually seems to know what he is talking about. Then I remember that he is drawing in *my* sketchbook.

"Excuse me," I snap and grab my sketchbook back from him.

"Hey, why'd you do that? I'm just trying to help. You obviously have talent, but you need—"

"The only thing I need to do is prepare for this audition," I tell him, although the fact that he just said my drawing shows talent does not go unnoticed. "You should put your time into preparing as well, rather than going around correcting other people's drawings."

He takes his hand and casually flips his hair away from his face. "I don't have to prepare."

"Oh? So is everything you do perfect?" I say with as cutting a tone as I can summon.

"Yep," he says. "Pretty much." I can't tell if he is joking or being serious. "But the truth is, I'm not here for the audition, or at least I am not here *to* audition."

I am about to ask him what the heck that means when Phoebe comes around the corner. I swear she has the timing of a psycho-killer in some slasher movie. Just when I have forgotten about her, she pops up again like a zombie that won't die.

"Hey, you!" she says, smiling and pointing at me. I guess it means another episode of *Let's Pretend to be Best Friends*. I hope I can stomach another one so early in the day. "I knew you would be here. I just knew it." She goes on about something, but I am barely paying attention as I am using this distraction to take a better look at this boy. I can admit that if he were not such a jerk, he would almost be all right. Then somehow I hear Phoebe say, "And I am glad you two are getting reacquainted."

"Reacquainted?" I ask. Sure, I saw him at the big-box store audition with Phoebe, but that was from a distance. You could barely call that an introduction. I don't think I've ever seen this boy before in my life. Have I?

"Brittany, you must remember my brother Liam."

I almost fall to the floor. There is no way the boy standing before me can be the same boy I used to see with Phoebe and her mother at auditions before I left for Hong Kong. The kid I remember who claimed to be Phoebe's brother had a short crew cut, glasses the size of small windows, skin that looked like a stick of melting butter, and he definitely shopped in the boy's husky department. The boy standing in front of me could be a model for any of those clothing stores where you see those black-and-white photos of guys running around without their shirts for some unknown reason.

"Hello, Liam," I say, unable to reconcile the image of the boy standing in front of me and my memory of the kid I knew a year ago.

"Yeah," he says. "I didn't think you remembered me. I used to go by William but it's Liam now. A lot can change in a year."

"It certainly can," I say.

For just a moment we are staring at each other, until Phoebe says, "Tell me about it," and laughs her strange sort of snorty elephant-laugh. "Until I started working with Liam on my auditions, and going over my lines with him, I hardly booked at all. He's like my coach and good luck charm rolled into one."

"He is?" I say. That explains a lot, like how she is able to book *anything*. Obviously having her brother around makes her less nervous and that has most likely been the reason why she has been able to start booking.

"Oh, yeah," Phoebe says. She goes on to tell me that she couldn't possibly book all of the work she gets without him. He goes with her to all of her auditions and helps her prepare, but also just helps her not get nervous. "He's not only my brother, he's also my best friend."

"See," Liam says. "Some people appreciate my help."

Before I can come back at him with some smart remark I hear, "Todd Sullivan and Brittany Rush!" A woman with a clipboard stands in the doorway to the studio and yells my name.

"Gotta go," I say as I quickly throw my sketchbook into my bag and raise my hand. "Brittany Rush. I'm right here." I sprint over to the door, and next to the woman with the clipboard is the boy I'll be auditioning with. He is cute but nowhere near the level of cuteness Liam has achieved. "Hey," he says and flips his head back just a bit. "I'm Todd."

"Brittany," I say as I walk into the room and smile at him. As I pass in front of him, I add, "Let's go book this, shall we?" moving my eyes to the side. I haven't really flirted with a lot of boys yet, but I figure there is no time like the present to start.

Todd turns out to be kind of lame. During the

audition he misses his cues and when he is supposed to hold my hand, he grabs it so hard I wonder if it might fall off. Still, I remain focused on my cues, and even though he is beaming a smile that is as forced as a little kid on school-picture day, I make sure my smile is pleasant and natural.

At the end of the audition we walk out of the room and before heading out, he turns to me and says, "See you at the callback, babe." I just nod my head without saying anything since the chances of that are slim to none.

Luckily, outside the studio is total chaos. The elevator has just dumped another herd of kids into the waiting area where they are signing in and looking for the sides. I see Phoebe and Liam sitting in a corner going over the sides. I wonder if she's right. I wonder if Liam really is her secret weapon.

After all, how would someone like Forgetful Phoebe go from being a nobody to my biggest rival in less than a year? This is the same girl who I personally witnessed at a callback where we were playing cheerleaders get so nervous that she forgot the word "team" came after the word "go." I think about this as I sneak out of the waiting area to the elevators, avoiding them both.

CHAPTER 13

That night I review my sketchbook like a scientist searching for the cure to a deadly disease. I examine every line of every drawing to see what I am missing. What did I have last year that I don't have now? When I was a kid going on auditions, I remember how strange it was to enter the rooms for the first time. Every girl looked a little like me. Some were a bit more sporty looking and others were a bit more glamorous, and even though there were differences in how we wore our hair or our physical features, back then we all looked a lot alike. Every time I opened the door to a waiting room at a casting office it felt like jumping into a sea of me, but when I look at my drawings I don't get that feeling at all. All of these girls have the same commercial look, but they are all different from one another. They look like individual pieces of the same puzzle.

It's a cool summer night so the windows are open and the air conditioning is off. I can hear the crickets outside. I walk out of the family room and onto the deck outside where I see the faint, orange glow of fireflies on the perimeter of the deck. For a second I think about running inside to get Christine and grab some empty jars so we can make firefly lanterns, but then I change my mind.

Christine is upstairs chatting online with her friends from Hong Kong. Last week she actually asked my parents if she could visit them for spring break next year with some of her new friends from soccer camp. That's Christine. She's probably doing more for world peace than Hillary Clinton. My parents actually thought it was a good idea and asked if I wanted to bring some friends and go with her. At first I thought they were kidding. Spring break is an ideal time to go out on go-sees as I don't have to worry about classes. The next time I step foot in Hong Kong it will be because I have booked an international campaign for some trendy new soft drink that's taking over all of Asia. Until then, I have no intention of going back.

I walk back in from outside, close the screen

door, and take a seat on the couch. It's time to stop daydreaming and get to work. I turn to a fresh page in my sketchbook and turn on the TV. I have the TV and family room to myself for the next hour or so. If I channel surf efficiently that should give me plenty of time to do my research. I quickly flip to MTV and when I find some mindless reality show, I start scanning the other channels until I find something useful. It doesn't take long.

I catch the tail end of an entertainment news show. The eerily skinny host says, "We'll be back with more celebrity scandals caught on videotape right after a break." Perfect. I sit up and poise my pencil on the sketchbook, ready to draw anything that might be useful. The first commercial is for a car dealership. These are almost always local spots and rarely feature kids. Local spots only air regionally so they have the lowest production values and usually involve the owner of the dealership screaming at the camera. Not something that will help me.

The next commercial is what is called a beauty spot. Beauty spots are a totally different thing than the commercials I audition for. Beauty spots are usually for cosmetics or some other product found in that area of the drugstore. They are usually cast with adult female fashion models who very rarely speak on camera. While these women may look like Greek statues, they often sound more like waitresses in a Greek diner. The next spot starts with a graphic for AppleTime drinks. Their campaign has been the same for years. A bunch of scenes of people doing exciting things, like rock climbing or sailing, and then the voice-over asks, "What time is it?" and the person doing the activity turns to the camera and says, "It's AppleTime!" I know this is marketed toward kids my age so I get my pencil ready.

The first image flashes on the screen and the shock of it makes me push so hard on my pencil that the point snaps. It's Forgetful Phoebe on my television set. She is sitting in front of a vanity pretending to put on makeup with her mother, while outside the house some boy is standing with a bouquet of flowers. The camera cuts back to Phoebe and her fake mom. Then the voice-over asks the question and Phoebe holds a bottle of the vile-looking beverage and says, "It's AppleTime!"

That just might be the stupidest commercial I have ever seen and that's taking into account the one where I played a talking tortilla chip on roller skates at the beach. Who the heck drinks apple juice before their first date? That makes absolutely no sense. I remind myself that I should not spend time trying to figure out the spot. They make sense to someone somewhere in the world and they certainly make sense to the client, so who am I to think otherwise?

I grab the remote and rewind the DVR to take a more careful look at Phoebe. I pause on a frame that features her alone in a medium close-up. The blue light of the TV fills the slowly darkening family room and I just sit and stare at the flickering image for a while, like that little girl in *Poltergeist*. I can't find the words to describe what I am feeling. I'm in shock, angry, jealous, outraged, but mostly confused, so I grab a new pencil without a broken tip from the side table and start to draw.

I hear Mrs. Bayer's words from art class in my head. *Tune everything else out and just use lines to recreate on paper what you see with your eyes. Your hands are connected to your mind*, she would say. Those were the only times I was happy in Hong Kong. When I was drawing, I was able to forget about everything else, just like Mrs. Bayer said. Focusing on these drawings allows me to feel the same way, almost like I am in a trance. The only thing that exists in the world is me and this paper and pencil in front of me. After a few minutes I put the finishing touches on the drawing and the trance breaks. I actually get up from the couch and walk away from the drawing to clear my mind so I can look at it objectively.

What is it that Phoebe has that makes her so bookable these days? She is not unattractive. In fact, she's pretty. But pretty isn't everything in the commercial business. Sure, if we were models looks would be ninety percent of the whole thing, but commercials are different. Commercial girls are not clothes hangers. You don't need to be beautiful, you just need to look likeable, which, I have found, is very different from actually *being* likeable. In many ways it's *much* easier.

Phoebe has a small nose and her smile is wide and open. I can see how we wind up at a lot of the same go-sees. Her hair is almost the same shade of blond as mine and we both have the same "look," but underneath her seemingly pleasant exterior is . . . well, actually more pleasantness. I release the pause button and fast-forward through the tail end of the commercial since I've gotten all I'll get from it.

I start to flip the channels and there she is again— PHOEBE! This time she's eating some type of breakfast pastry or something in a suburban kitchen with a fake mom, who I know very well. Margie Kruger has played my mom, like, a thousand times. Okay, maybe like half a dozen, but the fact is, Margie is mine. How dare Phoebe think she can just waltz in and take my mother away?

I am about to change the channel again when the next commercial starts and the silly AppleTime jingle begins to play. I can't bear to see Phoebe in another spot and I push the off button on the remote so hard I think it might be stuck in that position permanently. Ka-ching for Phoebe—at least three spots during prime time. She must be raking in the bucks. Meanwhile, I am trying to figure out my life.

Christine comes bouncing down the stairs and finds me sitting, staring at the dark screen of the television I just turned off. She must think I am really losing it but she doesn't mention it. Instead she says, *"Ni hao?"*

I say "hi" back in Chinese. *"Ni hao."*

Ever since we have been back, we have been throwing little bits of Chinese into our conversations. We both took Chinese class in Hong Kong and, while I never plan to go back, it's nice using the language with Christine. It's not exactly our secret language since billions of people speak it, but still it's something I only do with Christine.

"Hey, do we have any more of that green tea ice cream Mom bought at the Asian grocery?" Christine asks, walking into the kitchen.

"Yeah," I say. "And green tea ice cream sounds great right now." I could use a little pick-me-up and drawing and green tea ice cream are, like, the only two good things that happened to me in Hong Kong. I follow Christine into the kitchen. She pulls the ice cream out of the freezer and I get two bowls and spoons. The frozen green concoction tastes like nothing else in the world. It's sweet but also a little smoky tasting in this totally unexpected but delicious way.

"Hey, Britty, remember that kid Henry Wong from school in Hong Kong?" she asks.

"Ah, no," I say, taking a spoonful of ice cream.

"Sure you do. He had glasses and really long hair."

"Ah, no," I say again. Actually, I didn't make a lot of friends in Hong Kong. I'd like to think that was simply because I knew we would only be there for a year, but the truth is I don't have that many friends here in Great Neck. I've always been too busy with my auditions, and once you start appearing on television regularly it makes it harder to make friends.

"You have to remember him. His parents were like ga-billionaires. They owned that line of skin care stuff and all those cosmetics stores. You went to that big birthday party he had at Club Liquid, with all the balloons."

Of course, I remember that party. How could I not? His parents rented the entire four floors of Club Liquid and each floor had a different theme. It was pretty amazing but I only went because he was friends with Christine. I don't think he ever knew who I was. I spent a lot of the party just talking to his mother. Still, it was a cool party.

"Well," Christine says. "According to Akiko, who heard it from Yi-Chen, Henry's parents were so excited that he got a C-plus on his report card that they actually bought him a bright red VW bug convertible."

"No way," I say.

"I know! I mean, I don't know what is more shocking: that Henry actually passed a class or that his parents bought him a car when he's not even old enough to drive."

"Well, that C-plus must have been in gym," I say and Christine laughs.

"That's so funny," Christine says and laughs

harder. "I have to go upstairs and IM Akiko that you said that. Brit, the things you say. You crack me up." Christine bops out of the kitchen to go upstairs to IM her friends, but turns back to me before heading out. "Hey, Karen and Jaimie are coming by so we can go hang out downtown. If they ring the doorbell just send them up to my room, 'kay?"

"Sure," I say as Christine walks up the stairs.

It's incredible to me how her life has continued without any interruption. She left for a year but she might as well have just hit the pause button on the DVR of her life. Click. She hits it again and her life picks up at the exact same place as before she left. The only difference is that now she has friends in two different parts of the world. If it was anyone else but my sister, I'd be jealous.

Usually it doesn't bother me at all, but sometimes I wonder what it would be like to hang out with a bunch of friends who like the same stuff, instead of the instant friendships that are a result of some director's instructions. I guess hanging out with kids on camera is as close as I am gonna get, and lately it doesn't even look like I have that.

My cell phone rings and I don't even look at the number. I'm sure it's my parents checking in with me. "Hello," I croak into the phone, the sadness and depression flowing out of each syllable. I make a mental note to remember this tone in case I ever have to audition for an antidepression drug.

"Well, you don't sound very happy," the voice on the other end of the line says.

"Oh," I say, perking up. "Judith, what's up?"

"I'll tell you what's up. You have a callback for that amusement park spot. They want to see you tomorrow at . . ."

"Hold on," I say. "Let me get something to write with." I put the phone on the couch and reach for a pencil. All of a sudden nothing else in the world matters. I don't care about Phoebe or all of Christine's friends or Henry's new car. I want to book this spot and I *will* book this spot.

As I write down the information, I get a very good feeling. This is it. This one I am going to book. This callback will be the start of my comeback.

CHAPTER 14

At the initial audition for this spot, all the kids were chatting and goofing around with each other. A lot of the boys were being loud and obnoxious while a lot of the girls were giggling and gossiping. The audition was like any middle-school lunchroom you might find anywhere in the country. But this callback is serious. Everyone is studying the sides and I am no exception.

I look at each panel making sure I understand what they'll want me to do. The waiting area is still crowded since this spot needs a lot of people, but it is not nearly as full as the original audition. The director is seeing us in groups of eight, four boys and four girls. It is clear to see from the sides that two of the kids are the leads while the others are there to play the friends. I look around at the other girls and consider which ones I would want to be my friends. None of them look like great girl friend material to me, but in a pinch I'm sure some of them will do. As I look around the room I take special pleasure in the fact that Phoebe is nowhere to be found. I am about to breathe a sigh of relief when, from around the corner, I hear her voice shouting, "Liam? Liam, are you here?"

She walks into the waiting area, scanning the group, and then she sees me. I'm in no mood to interact with Phoebe at the moment. I need to prepare for this callback. Of course, she comes right up to me. "Brit, thank goodness you are here." Funny, I am having the exact opposite feeling about her. "Have you seen Liam?"

Great. As if dealing with her isn't enough, I am going to have to endure her obnoxious, albeit extremely cute, brother. I want to tell her I just saw him leave the building so she will wander aimlessly outside, but she seems to be in a mild panic so I just say, "Haven't seen him." I stare down at my sides, hoping she will take this as a clue to go away.

She doesn't.

"Liam said he would meet me here for the callback. He was going to some comic-book store and then meeting me here. He's not answering his cell phone. What am I going to do?" she asks, her anxiety escalating.

"I'm sure he'll be here by the time you get out of the callback." I say.

"No, no, no, no, no, no," she says, shaking her head back and forth. "You don't understand. I can't . . . go . . . I . . ." She stumbles over her words.

"Spit it out, Phoebe" I say, just staring at her. This is the girl who is actually booking spots over me. This girl, who can't form a sentence. Life is cruel and mysterious.

"I . . . I . . . ," she stammers, "get too nervous."

Well, my, my, my. Little Forgetful Phoebe has a bad case of the nerves without her big brother Liam to calm her down. I forgot how serious an issue this was for her until just now. I mean, I knew she often got nervous, but I hadn't remembered how it had almost prevented her from booking anything.

"Liam!" Phoebe shouts, and I turn to see Liam walking over to her.

For a split second I forget that he was so rude to me at the audition and that he is the brother of my biggest competition and only see the fact that the cutest boy in the room is walking right toward me. For that split second I see Liam as just another kid who likes to draw.

"Sorry, Phoebe," he says, and then when he sees

me, he smiles and says, "Hey, Brit. I had a feeling you would be here. Bring your sketchbook?" It's an innocent enough question, but I am not about to be distracted by Liam's charms when I am so close to booking my first spot since being back.

"Look, I really should go prepare," I say coldly. A fake mom once told me about an old deodorant commercial of hers where she faced the camera directly and said, "Never let them see you sweat." Since then I've always thought that was an excellent motto to live by. I am not about to let Phoebe or Liam see me as anything but camera ready. I grab my sides and find a quiet corner of the waiting area to review the scenes.

CHAPTER 15

The Long Island Rail Road platform at Penn Station is always about ten degrees hotter than the street above it. There is just no way to stay fresh and cool while waiting for the train back home. Luckily, it's a few hours before the rush and the platform is relatively empty. As the sweat builds on my forehead, I try to remember every detail of the callback I just finished.

I thought it went well, very well. The hardest part was trying to imagine the cramped casting studio was actually an amusement park with rides and games. At one point the boy buys the girl some cotton candy and we had to pretend that this disgusting, chewed-on pencil was actually a fluffy, pink mass of spun sugar. It was gross but I did my best to stay focused.

A few times they had me play the girl who gets the boy, the lead role. A few times they had me play one of her friends. This troubled me. I remind myself they had all of the girls rotate through the lead role so they were probably just being fair. Even Faith Willis got a chance at playing the girlfriend role, though there is almost no chance she'll book the part. She's cute and has the right look, but she was just trying way too hard with every take. You have to let them come to you a bit. If you seem too overeager you'll never book anything.

"Brittany! Brittany!" I hear from the other end of the platform. I don't even have to look over to see who it is. I know Phoebe is racing toward me without even looking in her direction. The only question is whether or not she has her personal good luck charm with her. "Hey there," she says a little out of breath. "I thought that was you. I was wondering if you would be on this train." The Markses live about ten minutes from us on the other side of Great Neck. They actually belong to the same swim club we do, which, I realize now, is one of the reasons I have been avoiding going there since I have been back. "Liam said you would be on this train, but you ran out of the callback so fast I didn't have a chance to ask you."

Very interesting. So Liam was talking about me.

He was probably telling her how my drawings lacked a good sense of perspective. I notice, however, that Liam is not with her. "Where's your brother?" I ask in my practiced nonchalance. My tone implies that I have no interest whatsoever in the answer; I am merely asking out of lack of anything better to do.

"He stopped at the newsstand upstairs to get some comic book that just came out, some new mango or something."

She couldn't possibly mean what I think she means. "You mean *manga*?"

"Oh, yeah. That's it, manga, whatever that is." She shrugs her shoulders as if she is describing Q-tips or tollbooths.

"Manga is, like, one of the coolest things ever. It's all bright colors and big, blocky graphics," I tell her but she is barely listening to me.

"Hey, I saw Rory Roberts go in the studio with you for the boyfriend role. I think Cassie has a crush on him. Isn't he the cutest boy you have ever seen or what?" she asks. She really wants an answer.

"Which one was he?" I ask. I don't add, "And who in the world is Cassie?"

"Which one was he?" she asks like I just asked her to saw off her own foot. "He was the cutest one there. He was wearing a red polo shirt. How could you miss him?"

"I remember him. He's okay." I say and now I'm the one shrugging my shoulders. I try to think back and see if I can remember what he looked like. The truth is, I barely pay attention to the boys at a go-see. I mean, they aren't exactly competing for the same parts I am. Now that she mentions it, I have to agree with her. Rory is cute, very cute. Maybe I should start paying more attention to the boys at my auditions, but that would mean getting distracted and I know that being focused is key to booking spots.

"I got it!" Liam says, walking toward us on the platform, holding up a thin, brown paper bag. He is about three inches taller than I am. If he were not related to my secret archnemesis, I might actually find him very attractive.

The train pulls into the station and, even though we're all used to the overwhelming noise, it still manages to put all action and conversation into suspended animation for a moment. The loud screech of the brakes signaling that the train has finished pulling into the station is followed by the futuristic swish of the train doors as they open automatically, allowing us to enter.

My plan is to get on the train after Phoebe and Liam, then quickly turn in the opposite direction they are headed so I will not have to endure thirty-five minutes of Phoebe's endless rattling punctuated by Liam's snide comments.

The conductor starts listing the towns where the train stops over the loudspeaker and Phoebe and Liam start to board. But before I even get my foot in the train door, Phoebe yells, "Hey, guys, over here. There is an open box!" A box is when the seats face each other. This train has three seats across and the box has three facing front and three facing back, which means I will not only have to listen to Phoebe, I will have to look at her as well.

The passengers behind me want to get to their seats so I don't have any time to think of an excuse as to why I cannot sit with them. Instead, I just move out of the aisle and plop myself in a seat next to Phoebe so at least I don't have to look at her. This does mean I will be forced to look at Liam, but since his physical features far outshine his personality, I believe I have made the right choice.

"All aboard!" the conductor yells. The doors shut and the train slowly makes its way out of the underground station and begins its slow ascent through the tunnel out of Manhattan. The train travels in darkness for a few minutes before exiting the tunnel. For some reason these minutes are always very quiet on the train. Few people talk and those who do, do so in very hushed tones.

Of course, Phoebe does not follow these obvious social norms. As soon as the train starts moving, she starts talking through the darkness. I'm learning that she will talk about anything. Within six minutes she goes from reality TV to a new lip gloss she is using to her friend Bonnie's horse at summer camp to a granola bar she ate the other day that tasted like strawberry even though the wrapper said raspberry. The train surges out of the tunnel into daylight, but this jarring action does little to interrupt Phoebe's monologue. "I mean why would they put strawberries in a raspberry granola bar? It just doesn't make sense. Are strawberries cheaper than raspberries? I don't think so and what if . . ."

Suddenly the sound of "La Vida Loca" starts coming out of her purse, but even this doesn't stop the stream of words coming out of her mouth.

"Phoebe," Liam says, "your purse is ringing." He points to the sequined, lime-green shoulder bag on her lap.

"Oh my gosh!" She fumbles through her purse to find her phone and I suddenly tense up.

If this is her agent calling to tell her she just booked something, I promise myself I will jump off this moving train or push her off it. I decide to make my final decision based on how big the spot it is. She looks at her phone and shouts, "It's Cassie." Good news: No one will be leaving the train before we actually arrive at a station. "Cassie!" she yells into the phone and Liam points to a sign above her head stating that cell phones are only allowed on every other car in the train. We happen to be riding in a cell phone–free car so Phoebe whispers into the phone, "Hold on," and then to us, "Sorry I HAVE to talk to her." Then she leaves her seat to go to the car behind us.

My immediate reaction is one of relief since now some other person is stuck listening to Phoebe for the next thirty minutes. However, this relief is quickly diminished by the fact that I am now sitting across from Liam without the buffer of his chatterbox sister. I consider making up an excuse to go sit somewhere else, but when I look around I see that the train is pretty full and, really, what kind of an excuse could I come up with for suddenly getting up and moving a few seats away to sit next to a total stranger.

I focus my gaze out the window hoping this will

prevent us from having any type of conversation. I watch the large urban warehouses that edge the rail yards give way to the apartment complexes and row houses that make up Queens, the official buffer between Manhattan and the suburbs of Long Island.

The sun is at the exact angle in the afternoon sky to allow me to catch a glimpse of Liam in the reflection of the window. I take some time to really look at his face since this vantage point allows me to watch without being seen. Gazing at the reflection I can almost remember how Liam used to look with his braces and super-short crew cut. I barely noticed him back then, but there is no way any girl would not notice him now with the braces off and his hair grown out. Still, it's not just the change in his physical appearance that is so different. There is something else.

I notice that he is staring down at his lap. At first I think he reading his new manga. I would be. Then I realize he actually has his sketchbook out; he's drawing. I turn from the reflection to look at him in person. Seeing the detail of his clenched lips and knit brow tells me he is frustrated by something. His hand dives into his bag and he pulls out a large, gray, soft-gum eraser, the kind that serious artists use. He starts rubbing it over the lower half of his drawing.

I tilt my head around to see what he is so furiously erasing. He is working on a really beautiful drawing of some sailboats in the harbor. I recognize the location as the harbor near Cliffside, which is a short bike ride away from the town we live in. His drawing is really amazing. He has captured the gentle rocking of the boats and the waves in the water perfectly. I have to admit, he knows what he is talking about in terms of perspective. The coastline starts off strong and rugged and then fades into the background before turning and going off the page.

However the bottom of the drawing has some issues, thus the eraser. He has the sun setting in the drawing so that means the shadows need to look a certain way. Shading was something I really excelled at in Mrs. Bayer's art class.

"You have them going in the wrong direction," I tell him and move over to sit next to him. I grab the pencil out of his hand and use the back of it to point at the drawing. "See, if the sun is here," I point off to an imaginary horizon, "then the shadows have to go like this." Again, I use the back end of the pencil to indicate a point on the drawing. This time I am moving the pencil in a direction opposite to the one he had the shadows going in.

"You're right," he says without a hint of attitude. It makes me wonder why I was so angry when he was trying to help me with my drawing. I should have just thanked him. He takes the pencil and starts drawing his shadows going in the direction I suggested and the whole picture begins to look more complete. He smiles as he works and I smile, too, although I tell myself to make sure I wipe the smile off my face when he finally looks up from his sketch.

When he finishes the shadows, he holds the drawing in front of him to examine it. "Thanks, Brit. That made a big difference."

"No problem," I say and turn my head to look out the window, hoping he will think I have actually been looking out the window the whole time rather than watching him.

"Are you like this with everything?" he asks.

"Like what?" I ask, not turning away from the window.

"You know . . ." he hesitates, looking for the exact word. "Confident," he finally says.

It's not the word I am expecting. I am expecting pushy or aggressive or difficult. I know that when I want something, I don't let anything get in my way.

The word "confident" makes me smile even though it doesn't exactly convey how I feel after today's callback. As a matter of fact, I feel a severe *lack* of confidence.

Liam opens his backpack and shuffles some things around before pulling out a single piece of paper that looks like it has been in his bag for quite a while. He nudges me and then hands me the bright blue piece of paper. "You should come to this, you know." I look at the paper and it looks somewhat familiar. It's the same announcement that my mom gave me a few weeks ago for the art stuff at the community center. "They have an afternoon class for advanced students taught by this guy I study with—Mr. Snyder. He teaches at Parsons in the city during the year and he really knows his stuff. "

"Oh," I say, taking the paper from him and looking at it.

"Registration ends next week. The class is filling up. You should really head over as soon as you can."

"Thanks, Liam. I appreciate it," I tell him, "but I am really focused on my career."

"I *know* how focused you are." He says, shaking his head at me and smiling. "I've never met another girl like you but, listen Brittany, Mr. Snyder really knows his stuff. He could help you with your perspective issue."

How dare he say I have an issue with perspective! "I don't have an issue with perspective!" I snap back at him.

"Whatever," he says, and rolls his eyes like I do when I am talking with my mother.

"No, not whatever. I don't have issues with perspective. Period."

"Okay, well, sign up for class and have Mr. Snyder take a look," he tells me with a tone of challenge in his voice.

"I don't need anyone to take a look at anything!" I am almost shouting now and a few people turn their heads to see what the commotion is. I quickly lower my voice but make sure my tone is deliberate. "Look, Liam. I take my career very seriously." I say the word seriously and slowly, breaking apart each syllable. "I don't have time to go to any random art classes at the moment. I have to put all my focus on my career."

He looks at me with a smirk and then mumbles, "Maybe that's the problem."

I pretend I didn't hear him even though I understood each word. Is he trying to tell me that I am too focused on my commercial career? That is just not possible. Having focus is what makes a career.

Isn't it?

CHAPTER 16

A booking.

I finally have a booking and it is an awesome one at that. I knew from the first moment I walked into that audition for the amusement park that I was going to book it. That's how it used to be. I would just get a feeling that I was going to book something and then I would book it. Judith was so happy for me when she called. We both knew this was the beginning of me making my way back to the top.

Taking the elevator up to the fitting, I feel even more excited. Maybe tomorrow when I'm actually on location I'll feel differently, but now I'm too pumped up. The shoot is on-location at the Seven Sails Park in New Jersey. They are closing the sections we are filming in, which means we will get to ride the rides over and over again with lots of people watching.

That might make me nervous, but today I am just excited since wardrobe fittings are one of my favorite parts of booking a job.

On a major shoot the wardrobe fitting takes place the day before the actual shoot at one of the costume shops on the west side of Manhattan. A costume shop is like a department store with stacks and stacks of clothes. However, instead of having twenty shirts in different sizes but all the *same* style, here there are twenty shirts in one size but all *different* styles. I'm headed to the Klein Costume and Wardrobe on West Fourteenth Street. It is one of my favorites since it's one of the largest.

When I arrive, the receptionist sends me to the back of the fitting room, which means I have to go through the wardrobe storage area, a place I would seriously dream about when I was living in Hong Kong. I open the heavy metal door and begin walking down the narrow aisle through this magnificent canyon of fashion.

The storage area is a huge warehouse with enough wardrobe in it to clothe a small- to medium-sized country. The racks and racks of clothing are precisely stacked on top of one another, like shelves in a giant bookcase. It looks a bit like a dry cleaner's since everything rotates at the push of a button, so higher shelves and racks can be lowered. But this place is fifty times the size of the largest dry cleaner's you have ever seen, and everything is organized so precisely even the biggest control freak would be impressed.

I walk very slowly through the racks and stop to look up at the area reserved for blue dresses. There must be hundreds of them in every shade from dark, almost black, navy blue to light powder blue to vibrant shades of aqua. Some look like they just flew in from a Paris runway, and others look like they are from the turn of the century, just waiting to be used in some period piece. They each hang, waiting to make an appearance in a commercial or an episode of a television show or the latest summer blockbuster. I guess they are like me in a way: just waiting for the next big booking.

Past the rack of blue dresses is a shelf of folded sweaters. I see the label, CARDIGANS, and look up toward the ceiling and figure there must be at least two hundred cardigan sweaters. A few look like the kind you might see an elderly teacher wear, while others are the kind a young mom would wear to pick up her kids from school. Each article of clothing has its own purpose and its own character.

I walk past rows of trench coats and shelves of scarves and then rows of nurse uniforms and shelves of ski hats. I can only image what are on the racks and shelves that extend back beyond the walkway into the walls of the building. I would love to be locked in here overnight like the kids in that book who sleep overnight at the museum.

Giving one last look to the storage area, I open the door to the fitting room. "Brittany, darling, how are you?" a slim man in his late twenties squeals as he runs over and gives me a hug. I hug him back and then we give each other an air kiss on each cheek.

"Channing, darling," I say with as dramatic a flair as he greeted me. "I was just praying you would still be here."

A chubby woman with jet-black hair teased into a beehive comes around the corner and says, "And what am I? Chopped liver? I fitted you for your first diaper, sweetie, don't you forget it."

"Doris!" I shout, and run over to give her a hug. I was hoping I would see both of them today but did not want to get my hopes up. I've quickly learned that a lot can happen in a year, and anytime I've been expecting things to still be the same as when I left, I am disappointed. It's nice to find that at least one thing hasn't changed.

"So, how was Hong Kong?" Channing asks. "I hear the kids there are very fashion-forward."

"Maybe," I tell him, "but I had to wear a uniform to school and most of the other kids I saw were from the States or the UK, so I wouldn't know."

"Chan, I missed our little Miss Brit just like you, but we've got enough fittings to keep us here until next month. Let's get moving," Doris says, and scurries to the back of the room.

"Oh, Doris," Channing tells her, "Cool your jets!" These two are always bickering. Some people would find it uncomfortable but I love it; I know this is how they work best together. "Anyway," Channing adds, "Brittany is a professional. She'll whiz right through this."

I smile broadly at good old Channing. After feeling like everyone in this entire town had forgotten who I was, it's nice to finally have someone recognize my professionalism.

Doris walks over to the worktable with her arms full of clothes. Channing goes to a box at his desk and pulls out my size card from the original audition.

Once you book a commercial, the size card goes immediately to the wardrobe crew, where they pull different looks they think will work for the shoot from the wardrobe warehouse.

"Let's start with this," Doris says and pulls out a lime-green-and-white striped tank and a pair of white capris. It's a cute outfit but I'm surprised by their choice. Frankly, this is the type of average, blend-into-the-background outfit I would expect one of the girls in the secondary parts to wear, not the lead. And the bright lime-green stripes are a bit much.

I keep my opinion to myself and take the outfit from Doris and go behind the curtain to try on. Everything fits perfectly. I come out from behind the screen and stand on the short pedestal in the middle of the room so they can examine. I have probably stood on this pedestal a hundred times and had them scrutinize every inch of my appearance.

"Looks good," Doris says.

Channing nods his head but then scrunches his nose. "Wait a minute, white capris?"

"What? It's before Labor Day?" Doris says, ready to get into it with Channing again.

"But at an amusement park. Who would wear

white to an amusement park? It's like a carnival for stains," Channing says. I almost giggle, but stifle it instead and make sure I stay still. Part of being a professional is letting them do their job without interruption.

"You're right," Doris says. "Let's snap it anyway and go to the next one."

Channing grabs his digital camera and I stand looking straight forward. He takes a picture and, without needing him to give me any direction, I turn to show my profile and pause. He snaps a picture. Finally, I stand with my back toward him and he takes the final picture. These pictures all go to the director to show him what I look like in each option.

I hop off the pedestal, Doris hands me the next outfit, and I step behind the screen to try it on. This one is a gauzy, ballet-pink top with a scoop neck and small blue flowers embroidered on the sleeves. The hanger also has a pair of denim shorts. The whole outfit is super cute and I secretly hope they pick this one. This is the perfect outfit for the lead in a commercial, not that garish green thing.

I don't have a say in the final outfit, although a lot of times they ask me what I prefer or what I would wear if I had to choose. It means a lot to me that they respect my opinion, but Judith has always told me that I should only offer my opinion if I am asked. She says that kids who offer opinions without being asked are precocious, and precocious kids don't book.

I come out from behind the screen and stand on the pedestal. Channing and Doris quibble, then one of them takes out the camera. *Snap. Snap. Snap.* Then back behind the screen with another outfit. I do this for about half a dozen outfits but none of them are as cute as the one with the embroidered flowers on it. Not by a long shot. You actually don't know what you will be wearing until the day of the shoot and you find your wardrobe sitting in your dressing room. That's always an exciting moment. Seeing your wardrobe all pressed and folded, waiting for you, like a present on your birthday.

I step behind the screen again, this time changing back into my own clothes. I finish tying my sneakers on the other side of the screen so I can hang out with Channing and Doris a little bit longer.

Channing is going through a rack of boy's clothes and says to Doris, "Are there any more looks we need to pull for the boys? We have all three of them coming in next. Right?"

"Yikes," I say, pretending to be nervous. "I don't

want to run into the kid playing my boyfriend before the shoot. It might be bad luck, like the groom seeing the bride before the wedding ceremony." Channing laughs at my joke and Doris smiles for a second but then looks down at her size cards.

"Um, sweetie, *your* boyfriend? I have here that there are three girls playing friends and one girl playing the lead who meets the boy," she says slowly and carefully, as if I didn't go to both the audition and the callback.

"Yeah, I know," I tell her. Then there is a silence that starts off uncomfortable and quickly moves to awkward.

"Well," Doris finally says, "whatever happens tomorrow have a good time and enjoy yourself. We are just so glad to have you back."

I don't exactly understand what she is talking about, but I give her and Channing a hug and head out the door so they can start working on the next fitting. What did she mean by "whatever happens tomorrow"?

Tomorrow is the beginning of my comeback and I can't wait for it to arrive.

CHAPTER 17

On the day of a shoot I simply shower and comb my hair. I look awful and put on a wide-brimmed hat and a pair of sunglasses. I would usually never leave the house without doing my hair and putting on a little bit of makeup, but the day of a shoot I need to be a blank canvas—clean like a page in my sketchbook before I start to draw. There are professionals whose job it is to make me look great on camera. As I take a look at my pale face and lifeless hair in the mirror before I leave, I can almost hear Judith's voice in my head, *Let them do their job and you just do yours.*

My dad drives me into the city to meet the van that will take us to the location shoot. In the past I had someone accompany me during shoots, but my parents have finally decided to let me do these on my own. There is always someone on set anyway, making sure we don't get overworked and we finish our homework when school is in session, so my parents don't worry too much.

When I get in the van, I see two other girls my age who must be playing my friends. One I recognize from the callback, an Asian girl with short bangs and a wide smile. I can tell that she has curled her hair and is wearing makeup. Looks like someone is a newbie. Well, she'll learn once the hairstylist on set makes her take off all her makeup and shampoo her hair. The other girl has strawberry-blond hair and looks like she gets cast in the best friend role a lot. She has on no makeup but I can't tell if that is strategic or just a coincidence. I wave hello to them and try to give a friendly smile. I'm sure they were hoping to get cast in the lead and I hope they don't hate me too much for getting the role over them. I wonder where the other girl is but figure they must have cut her part. I take a seat in the front of the van and as soon as I sit down, I fall asleep.

We arrive at the amusement park hours before it opens and the whole place has a kind of a creepy feeling. It's strange to see a place that usually contains so much life totally still. The van drops us off at a back entrance where the camera crews and lights are already set up. There are the usual trailers as well: ones for dressing rooms, makeup, wardrobe, and a bunch of trailers for production equipment I never need to bother with.

We get out of the van and a woman in jeans and a T-shirt with her hair pulled back by a baseball cap comes out to greet us. "Hi," she says, "I'm Shirley and I'm the PA in charge of minors today, so if you have any problems, or you make any problems, I'm the one you'll be in touch with." She says the last part with a crooked smile, hoping we won't take offense. I don't. I've seen kids almost shut down entire productions because they were misbehaving. I'm sure Shirley has seen it all.

Shirley looks down at her clipboard and then points to each of us. "You are Jasmine, Cassie, and Brittany." We each nod when she says our name. "Great. The boys are in the next van and the other two kids are already in makeup." She says the last part under her breath but I hear every word. What does she mean "other two kids"? All three of us are standing in front of her. Could she mean the extras? Certainly there would be more than two extras, and why would they get here before us? I start to get a nervous feeling in my stomach.

"The call sheet is just past the craft services tent and behind the wardrobe and makeup trailers. The dressing rooms are in the trailer behind those. After you sign in, head over to craft services if you are hungry and then straight over to wardrobe and then to makeup. We need you on set A, by the merry-go-round, in exactly . . ." Shirley punches her wrist out from under her shirt sleeve. "Thirty-eight minutes."

The three of us start walking toward the location of the call sheet. The craft services tent looks amazing with piles of Danishes, fresh cut fruit, granola bars, and, of course, candy. Every set has a craft services tent which is on-set talk for the place where you can pig out. Producers don't want people wandering away from the set looking for something to eat, so craft services is like a portable restaurant with every kind of food you can imagine. I remind myself that Skittles are not a major food group and I should only eat them in moderation.

We walk past the wardrobe trailer and, even though the door is shut, I imagine Channing or Doris is behind it doing a last minute hem or sewing on a button. The door to the makeup trailer is open, and I let the two other girls go ahead of me to sign in so I can peek into the makeup trailer and see what two other kids Shirley has been talking about, since her mention of them made me a bit nervous. I poke my head into the trailer without going in and before I can even register my shock, I am attacked.

"Brittany!" Phoebe yells, and hops out of the makeup chair, leaving a confused makeup artist holding an eyebrow pencil up to thin air. This can't be. This just can't be. My first booking since I have been back and Phoebe has to be booked on it also. Of all the girls in the world *she* has to be playing my friend?

She gives me one of her trademark hugs, like I am a giant tube of toothpaste and she is trying to get the last bit out. I react as a tube of toothpaste would, lifeless and spent. I look around the trailer and I see a boy sitting in the makeup chair next to the one she just hopped out of. Wait. This is not looking good.

"I'm so excited," Phoebe says. "When I saw your name under mine on the call sheet, I thought, *This is just like old times.*"

She said the word "under." I am pretty sure she said she saw my name *under* hers on the call sheet. This cannot be happening. The call sheet lists the performers in order of importance. The leads are above the supporting roles and the supporting roles are above whoever is beneath that. If her name is above mine that means she is playing the girlfriend and I am playing *her* friend.

How in the world is this like old times?

It would be like old times if my name were on the top of the list and her name was on a piece of paper that was hanging a few inches from the floor, or if I were in that makeup chair while she was home practicing her accordion or whatever vile musical instrument takes up her free time.

Phoebe is still talking but everything she says is a blur, like her voice is coming out of a cell phone in a dead zone. I am not even close to paying attention. "Phoebe," I say without even looking at her, "I have to go sign in. I'll see you on set." I step off the stairs and walk toward the call sheet with fierce determination. I would run, but this would cause a commotion, and I don't want to call attention to myself. I walk around the trailer until I see the production table. I spot a clipboard on the end of the table and know it must have the call sheet attached. I walk over and grab it.

There in black and white is my worst nightmare.

CHAPTER 18

I drop the clipboard back on the table like it's a piece of barbed wire on an electrified fence. I stare down at the call sheet and there, directly ABOVE my name, is "Phoebe Marks—LEAD—girlfriend." To make matters worse, next to my name is the word "supporting." "Supporting" is such an ugly word. It makes me want to hurl.

I am truly in shock. I wonder if there is some mistake and I go to pull out my cell phone from my bag to call Judith. Judith will clear this up in a minute. Then I realize it is only 7:30 in the morning and Judith won't be in the office for another few hours.

I try to remember the phone call when I got the booking. I was so excited to get the booking that I don't remember her actual words. Perhaps she did say I was playing the role of the friend and I was so excited

I didn't take in what she was actually saying. That must have been what happened, since I am staring at the call sheet and it doesn't lie. For a second I imagine myself running after the van begging the driver to take me home. Instead, I walk to my dressing room. At least I have my own dressing room.

The dressing rooms on a trailer are usually very, very tiny. There is enough room for a chair, a vanity, and some sort of small couch that most people take naps on in between scenes. I shut the door and look at my watch. There simply isn't enough time for a good cry so I put down my bag and decide to be the young professional I know I am. Hanging on the back of my dressing room door is my wardrobe for the day in a black garment bag with my name written on it. I take the bag off the hook and lay it on the couch so I can unzip it. I only get the zipper a few inches down and I immediately know this day is about to get even worse.

Bright lime-green stripes blind me.

Where is that adorable outfit with the embroidered flowers? I'm sure Channing and Doris tried to convince some producer or director away from this sad excuse for a costume. Sometimes at the last minute there is a costume change, and as I put on the horrible, striped loser uniform, I pray that someone on set will come to their senses and go to the wardrobe trailer and pull a new look.

The speaker mounted in the ceiling crackles and someone announces, "I need supporting talent in makeup. Jasmine, Cassie, Brittany, Michael, Stephen, and Rory in makeup. All supporting talent in makeup. I need my leads, Phoebe and Doug, on set. Leads on set. Thank you."

How does one prepare for one of the worst days of his or her life? It's hard to ignore the fact that I have been replaced by Phoebe Marks when, not only do I have to work with her all day, but also the news is broadcast over loudspeakers at regular intervals. I wish there was time to take out my sketchbook and use my new charcoals to capture my mood at the moment. Drawing might even take my mind off the tragedy I am about to experience.

I walk robotically over to the makeup trailer. While we are getting our makeup done, I avoid making chitchat with the other *supporting* talent. Since we are going to be shooting outside, the foundation makeup is a little heavier than usual. At least Marco, the hairstylist for the day, pays special attention to my hair. He weaves a ribbon into a braid that falls down the center of my back. I look over at the other girls and see that their hairstyles are pretty simple. I'm grateful to have one thing to help me stand out.

After we finish makeup, we are ready for filming—but any film set is all about waiting. You wait for the lights, wait for the camera, wait for the set to be finished. The amount of preparation that goes into a filming a thirty-second spot is amazing. I sit with Jasmine and Cassie in an area behind the production equipment while we wait to be called on set to do some blocking.

"Phoebe is so lucky." Jasmine says.

I nod my head without saying a word.

"She gets to kiss Doug."

"Over and over again," Cassie chimes in with a sigh.

"He is such a hottie. If Phoebe needs a stand in, I'll be happy to help out," Jasmine says, and she and Cassie both giggle. Personally I don't see what all the fuss is about. Doug is cute, he might even be a hottie, but kissing him for a scene is just work. It doesn't mean anything.

"Moving on to scene D slash eight!" a production assistant with a megaphone announces. Shirley comes over to see if we need anything and then escorts us through the park to the next set. All of the rides are going and the colored lights are flashing even though the crew for the commercial is the only sign of life in the park at this hour of the morning.

When we get to the carousel, there is a huge lighting kit attached to one of the poles on the ride and a camera mounted to one of the horses. The crew is in the process of moving the camera and light kit for the next shot when the director comes over to us. He is a short, pudgy guy with a baseball cap. I know it is a stereotype that all male directors wear baseball caps but the fact is, it's true. Almost all male directors wear baseball caps. It must be in their contract somewhere.

"Good morning, girls," he says as he takes a sip of coffee from his stainless-steel travel mug. "I'm very pleased to have each of you here. This scene is very simple. You are watching your friend ride the carousel with this boy that you have been bumping into all day at the park. So let's have you on that mark and the other two on each side." He points for me to stand on the mark, which is just a piece of yellow tape on the ground in the shape of an X. The other two girls are on each side of me. At least I am in the center. That's good.

"So just hold those positions while we finish

the camera setups." He backs up and then does that thing directors do with their hands to make it seem as if they are looking through a frame. He smiles and shouts back, "Great, you girls look great."

We wait while standing on our marks. Luckily it is early enough in the morning that it is not too hot so our hair and makeup does not really mess up. There are assistants on set to primp us before the cameras actually start rolling.

After some time, the director uses the megaphone to clear the set. The carousel starts spinning again, the lights turn on us, and the director yells, "Action."

In an instant I make my mood of anxiety and frustration, disappear. *Poof.* I am just a girl hanging out with her best friends at her favorite amusement park. My face, my body, my whole being, is a bundle of friendship and happiness. I giggle with Cassie and whisper to Jasmine as we watch our other best friend ride the carousel with the boy she has been crushing on all day. The director yells, "Cut!" and *poof* I am back to being the disgruntled and confused girl I was this morning. The director makes some adjustments to the lights and again yells, "Action!" *Poof.* I am again that friendly girl you would love to hang out with until, *poof*, I am back to just being me.

After we finish the scene, the crew begins to set up for the next shot. I step off set and tell Shirley I am going over to the craft services table to get something to eat. Usually I would stay on set in between takes just to hang out with the crew or other talent, but I am in no mood to hang out with anyone. I know I told myself I would go easy on the Skittles today, but once I get to the craft services table, I start shoving them in my mouth like I'm in an eating contest. I have about a dozen in my mouth when I hear the shriek.

"Brittany!" Phoebe yells, and I prepare for one of her unbearable hugs that make me feel like my liver is going to pop out of my mouth. She releases me from the hug and says, "I'm so excited that we are working together again. Isn't this great?"

I finally raise my head to look at her and then I suddenly realize what she is wearing. She has on my ballet-pink top with the little, blue embroidered flowers and denim shorts. I start choking on my candy so hard I actually need to grab a napkin from the table to spit it out.

Phoebe pats me on the back a few times and asks, "Are you o-okay?"

"Yeah, I'm fine," I say, but the truth is I am anything but fine. I am hurt, confused, and angry. Who does Phoebe Marks think she is? First she steals my part in the commercial. Then she steals the wardrobe I wanted to wear. I make my mind up right then and there. Phoebe Marks must be stopped before she takes over my career completely. I have got to get her out of the way and steal something from her.

But what?

"You've got a twenty minute break," Shirley says as she walks by our table.

"Cool," Phoebe says, "Hey, Brit, you wanna go see what Doug and the other kids are doing?"

"You go," I say as I start walking away from her. "I'll be in my trailer."

I open the narrow door to my dressing room and go directly to my backpack to pull out my sketchbook and the new charcoal I have been working with. The last thing in the world I want to do is hang out with Phoebe on set. Drawing will help take my mind off the disaster that is my life. As I open my sketchbook, a bright blue piece of paper falls out and onto the floor.

"Yes!" I shout, because as soon as I see the piece of paper I know exactly what I have to do. It might take a little bit of hard work and an incredible talent for persuasion to pull it off, but those are two areas I just happen to excel in. A million thoughts race through my mind, but I quickly realize I need to stay focused if my plan is going to work. I unfold the blue paper carefully and take a deep breath before reading it closely and developing my plan.

Phoebe may think that after a year she can just become me and steal all of my bookings, and even my wardrobe, but she's underestimated me. I've figured out something I can steal from her, and it might just be the thing that helps me become *me* all over again.

CHAPTER 19

I burst into the house at full speed.

During the van ride back home from the shoot, I carefully reread the blue flyer announcing the advanced studio summer art classes at the youth center downtown, and realize that I need to get my plan in motion BEFORE six o'clock this evening since that's when registration ends. I know Liam is taking the class with Mr. Snyder this summer. If I can just get into that class, I will have enough contact with Liam to get him to like me. That should be enough to send Forgetful Phoebe into a stupor. Her fiercest rival dating her brother, who just also happens to be her secret weapon. Not to mention the fact that getting close to Liam means I might be able to get some dirt on Phoebe in case I need to mount a surprise attack. All I'll need is just one date with him and I'm sure

Phoebe will flip out. The very thought of it makes me smile.

My plan is brilliant, if I do say so myself. All the other plans I came up with during the drive back, like shaving Phoebe's head bald or dying her skin blue or rubbing a frog on her face so she breaks out in warts, were too physically demanding. The key to taking Phoebe down is cutting off her supply of confidence. Once I've taken care of that, it will be good-bye Lucky Phoebe and welcome back Forgetful Phoebe. For a second I get caught up in the fantasy of it all, but I quickly snap out of it since I am fighting a deadline.

If I miss the registration for class it means I won't have a chance, but I'll need some assistance from my parents to set the whole thing in action. I run into the kitchen and my mom is working on her laptop, surrounded by papers.

"Brittany, sweetie" she says, closing her laptop, "How was the shoot?" Not a good sign. When she closes the lid to her laptop it means she wants to have a conversation and I don't want to have a conversation right now, I just want to get her permission and some cash. "Or wait, I think you call it a shot. No, wait. Oh, I can't remember. Is it called a shoot or a shot?"

"It's called a shoot," I tell her, "And it was fine."

"Oh, I'm glad," she says. "Tell me all about it. Was Deveanna that makeup artist there? I remember her from when I used to have to be with you on set. She was going to have a baby then, but I guess her child must be a toddler by now. You know, I should e-mail her."

"Yeah, Mom, you should." I say, trying to quiet her. "Anyway, I wanted to ask . . ."

"Do you have her e-mail? Oh wait, I think I have it somewhere." She starts to open her laptop.

"Mom! I have to ask you something!" Once she re-opens her laptop, forget it. I'd have to be on fire to get her attention, and probably at full blaze, not just a few flames.

"I'm sorry, dear. What is it?"

"Can I still register for that art class at the center?"

"But I thought you were worried art class would interfere with your go-sees?" she asks.

"It's only a few hours a week and I can work it out with Judith. Please, Mom, please," I beg.

"I'm glad to see you so interested in drawing again," she says.

Of course, my motivation for signing up for these classes has nothing to do with drawing per se so her comment throws me for just a second, but I quickly recover. "Drawing, yeah, drawing. Oh, boy, am I excited to go back to drawing."

"I'll talk to your father tonight and you can register tomorrow."

"No, Mom. The registration ends tonight!" I look down at my watch "In, like, forty-two minutes. If I miss the registration I won't be able to sign up until the fall classes start." If she goes to her purse and grabs a check at this very moment, I might be able to get downtown in time to register.

"Well," she says, getting up from the table. "With Christine going to soccer camp during the day, I don't see why you shouldn't have something of your own to do. I'm sure your father will agree." She grabs her purse and takes out a checkbook, explaining that this check is only to be used to register for class, like I am someone going to use it to finance a Nigerian prince or something.

I grab the check and basically run the eight blocks to the community center downtown. I am desperate to make it to the center before registration ends. I burst through the double doors and see an older woman standing in front of a card table at the side of the lobby, putting some papers in a folder.

"Reg . . . regis . . ." I pant. The eight blocks have

really taken their toll on me and I can barely get the words out. The woman looks at me with a puzzled look.

"Excuse me, dear?" she asks, but does not stop cleaning up her papers.

I take a deep breath in and finally say, "Registration. I am here for registration."

She smiles at me and says, "I'm sorry. I just closed the books." She picks up her folders and begins to walk away.

"Wait!" I scream. "I need to register for Mr. Snyder's class this summer." I can tell my plea is not really making her change her mind, so I add, "It's a matter of life and death."

This gets her. She turns around and looks at me over her reading glasses. "How is an *art class* a matter of life and death?" she asks very slowly, as if she knows I was just being dramatic.

"Well," I say. "You see . . ." Each word comes out very slowly so my mouth has something to do while my mind is thinking of something. Then an idea pops into my head. "You see, my parents are thinking of getting a divorce and if I take this class, they will be able to go to counseling while I'm in class. It might save their marriage."

My parents have never once mentioned divorce and the very thought of either of them in something as touchy-feely as therapy makes me want to laugh out loud, but my little story seems to do the trick. She turns back to the table and sits herself down.

"Too many kids being shuttled back and forth between two parents," she says. "Which class did you want?" She opens her folders on the table.

"Mr. Gary Snyder's Studio Art Class," I say.

She shuffles a few papers and then looks up at me with a frown. "Oh, I'm afraid that class is full. Has been full for a while."

No problem. I wasn't cast as the girl who cried every time her daddy went away on business and his cell phone didn't get a signal for nothing. Most commercials traffic in happiness, excitement, and overall joy, but there are the rare examples that need a certain amount of anguish and despair, so one always needs to be ready to cry on cue. I look this sweet old woman right in the eye and let a single tear fall down my left cheek. As soon as she sees it, her frown turns into a sympathetic smile.

"Well," she says, "I don't think anyone will mind if I add just one more to this list." She erases something and then scratches something out. She tells me the fee and helps me make out the check, and just like that I am the newest student in Mr. Gary Snyder's art class. "Here is the list of materials you'll need," she says, handing me a small slip of paper. "Classes start in a week and," she lowers her voice, "good luck to your parents."

"Thank you," I tell her. "Thank you for everything." This woman may be thinking she has just saved a marriage, but she may have actually just saved something much more important—my career.

CHAPTER 20

I'm sitting in the kitchen eating a bowl of cereal, waiting to take the train into the city with my mom. My dad is watching the morning news and my mom is focused on her BlackBerry. I only have two auditions scheduled for the next week. Judith assured me this is only due to the fact that things are always slow at this point in the summer, and I have nothing to worry about since all of the big campaigns, including the Super Bowl ads, will start up after the holiday. I'm not worried. Not anymore. I've been going over my plan in my head and, theoretically, it should work.

"Brit, let me just finish this last e-mail and we'll head to the train," my mom says to me. Then she shouts in the general direction of Christine's bedroom, "Chrissy, if you want a ride to soccer today then you need to be down in here in under five minutes. I'm not kidding."

"I'm leaving, too," Dad says, getting up from the table.

He grabs the remote to turn off the TV just as a morning news host says, "We'll be back after these messages."

"Dad!" I shout. "Leave it on. The commercials!"

"Oh, right. Sorry, dear." He kisses me on the forehead and my mom on the cheek and leaves for work. He always forgets that the only things worth watching on TV are the things that happen in between the programs.

The first commercial uses animation. I hate commercials that use animation since that means it doesn't use any on-screen talent. Sure a few people got voice-over work in some audio booth somewhere to read the lines you hear, but no one recognizes you on the street unless you are talking on your cell or something.

The next commercial begins and I drop my spoon into my cereal bowl. It's me. It's not some imitation of me with my haircut and sassy attitude. It's actually *me*. I shot the commercial for Oats2Go breakfast bars about fifteen months ago. It was one of the last ones

I shot before we left for Hong Kong. In the commercial I am running through the kitchen on my way to school when my fake mom asks me what I want for breakfast. I'm too busy to decide and I say, "Oh, oh, oh, oh, Oats2Go." She hands me a bar, I take a bite and smile, and we both laugh.

What I remember about the shoot is having to eat, like, three thousand Oats2Go bars. They aren't bad, but after the tenth one, I was sick of them and we were only halfway through the shoot day. Kathy Silverman played my mom that day. I love working with her because she treats the kids just like she would any of the other talent on set. She never asks stupid questions like, "Do you enjoy playing pretend with all these cameras around?" I think I've been in three or four different commercials with Kathy. She played my mother once before in a different spot, and once she was my homeroom teacher.

Seeing myself on the small television makes it all come back to me—the feeling of being surprised by this image that is totally unexpected, but also totally familiar. I think about all the kids and families in their kitchens right now watching TV and seeing my face in between whatever program they are watching. I'm in their kitchens, their living rooms, their bedrooms.

Their eyes may not be glued to their television screens while my commercial is on, but they see. They definitely see me.

Christine walks into the kitchen, her hair still wet from the shower I am sure she took less than thirty seconds ago. She is just in time to catch the last few moments of the commercial where I say my big "Oh, oh, Oats2Go!"

"Hey, Mom, look! It's Brit in that granola bar commercial!"

My mom looks up quickly from her BlackBerry and sees the very last moments of me on screen. "Oh, Brit, I love the way they did your hair in that one."

"Yeah, it looks so cool. Can you show me how they did it?" Christine asks.

"Oh shoot! I wish your dad hadn't left. He would have loved to have seen this one again."

For the next few seconds, I don't care that half of the country is watching me. I'm just enjoying that most of my family is seeing me and asking questions about the shoot. They have seen me on TV hundreds of times, but it's been awhile since the TV version of myself just suddenly popped into our lives without warning. It's nice to just sit in the kitchen eating breakfast and suddenly see myself again. I know that girl on the TV so well.

I think I know her better than I know myself.

"Look at the time. Girls, we better go," Mom says, turning off the TV and grabbing her keys off the counter. I wonder how much longer it will be until my face starts popping up in the middle of breakfast on a regular basis. I follow my mom and sister out to the car.

On the train ride into the city, my mom works on her BlackBerry and I try to review my plan for getting my life back, but I can't stop thinking about seeing my commercial this morning. I can't imagine what it would be like to stop feeling that way.

What would it be like to just live my life like any other girl? To just be invisible?

I can't let that happen.

The way to take Phoebe down is to get close to her. Find out what she did while I was gone that turned her from a dull, unbookable girl at auditions into someone who books every single go-see she goes on. How did she go from being her to being me? Of course, dealing with Phoebe directly would be impossible. I would seriously wind up in a juvenile detention facility. The key to getting to Phoebe is Liam. Even she said she relies on him like a personal manager. If I can get close to Liam I can figure out how to bring Phoebe down. Signing up for the same art class as Liam means I'll be spending a few hours with him each week.

As usual, I'm early for my go-see at Mel Bethany's office. I sign in and am given a blank piece of paper and a fat Sharpie marker. I write the number that corresponds to my line on the sign-in sheet in big, bold print on the blank piece of paper. This is only something that happens at print auditions. I take my sign and go sit down to wait.

I hate being early at Mel's since the only place to sit is the long metal bench that lines the wall of the studio. This is a go-see for a print ad so there are no sides to look at or memorize. Each girl will just go in and stand in whatever ridiculous position they need and emote whatever feeling they want.

I'm wearing my frilly Priscilla top as this is an ad for a new line of sparkly school notebooks for girls, and whenever something is girlie, I bring out Priscilla. Luckily, she still fits. I look around the room before taking out my sketchbook and notice something very strange: Everyone is wearing a top that is some variation of Priscilla. Some have more ruffles and others are more sheer, but each of them could be related to

Priscilla in some way. We also are all wearing light-colored pants and have the same haircut more or less. Our hair is smooth and straight and falls just above our shoulders. No one is wearing a ton of makeup but everyone has on just a touch of color. There are six girls waiting to go in, including myself. We are split evenly on the two benches that face each other, and it looks like we could be staring into a mirror.

There was a time when I was the girl who stood out. The one everyone knew would book the spot. Now I can't figure out if I look like everyone else or if everyone else looks like me.

Go-sees for print ads are much quicker than commercial auditions since there is no video camera to set up or lines to run through, so girls come in and out of the studio pretty quickly. A woman pops her head out the studio door and yells, "Eight thirty-two!"

I get up from the bench and wave my number at the woman. The ink is still fresh and I can smell the Magic Marker fumes. I walk into the studio and go directly to my mark, a small, black T made with tape on the floor in front of the camera and lights but a few feet away from the sky-blue backdrop. About the time I learned to stand, I learned about the two types of marks used at auditions. There is the X, which means that you put yourself over the center of the mark. The T mark is slightly more complicated, as you put your toes at the line across the top of the T and straddle the long, vertical part with both feet.

I place my feet perfectly in line with the T and hold my number in front of my chest. A short man with lime-green glasses stands behind the camera, and one assistant holds a light while another is doing something on a laptop. The photographer sees that I am in the exact position he needs, yells "Great!" and snaps my picture. The assistant working the lights hands me a clipboard, and the photographer says, "Okay. Here is what we are doing today: You are a girl superhero and your new notebook gives you superpowers so you can run through school at lightning speed. I need to see three of your best superhero running poses."

I nod my head and smile, wondering why in the world running fast would be a useful superpower. Even X-ray vision beats speed running, but whatever. I take the clipboard and place it under my arm and lift my right leg up, like I am about to leap over something, and freeze in position with a determined smile on face.

The camera snaps and the photographer says,

"Great!" It doesn't mean I am doing a great job; it just means he wants me to go to the next pose. They always utter some affirmative catchphrase as long as what you are doing is passable. For the next one I throw my arms behind my back, like I am moving so quickly the wind has forced them behind me.

"I love it!" he says, and this time I think he actually means it. It's an uncomfortable position to hold very long, but I bet it looks cool in the lens. "Let's try a leap in the air on three. One, two . . . ," he says, and I begin bending my legs so I will have enough spring in them to be as high in the air as possible. "Three!" he shouts, and I leap in the air, my face a happy mix of ease and determination. "Excellent! Again. One, two, and three!" On command, I jump in the air. This time my expression is bolder, my leap grander. The photographer goes to check the images in the laptop and says, "Great work. Thanks, Brit." I smile and head out the door, but before I go, he asks, "Oh, who's your agent again?"

This is the one and only thing that can be said during a casting that actually means something good. "Judith Lister, of the A-Lister Agency," I say slowly and clearly so I am sure he understands every syllable. During a go-see, people love to heap praise on you. Photographers and casting directors always say things like "I love it" or "That was perfect" or "You are so good." I have learned to completely ignore the praise that happens in the studio. However, when someone asks you about your agency, it usually means they are seriously considering using you. It's the only thing that actually means anything. I walk out of the studio smiling to myself. Maybe things are about to turn around.

"Brit!" Of course, she's here. She's always here.

I brace myself for the horrible hug. She wraps her arms around me as her brother, Liam, looks on. Usually seeing the gruesome twosome would automatically put me in a bad mood, but today it doesn't bother me quite so much because I have finally figured out a way to get Phoebe out of my way.

"Phoebe, darling, how are you? It's wonderful to see you," I say with as much conviction as I would if I were at a go-see for a toothpaste commercial.

"Was that shoot at Seven Sails fun or what?" she asks.

"Or what," I say, making sure a solid smile is plastered across my face.

"Could you believe we had to do the kiss scene so many times? How many takes do you think we did?"

"Oh, I don't know," I say, remembering how it

felt to be on the sidelines with someone else in the spotlight. "Maybe three thousand."

Phoebe laughs some sort of weird horse laugh even though my comment was supposed to be biting, not humorous.

"Phoebe," Liam says, "you better sign in and see if there is anything you need to go over before you go in."

Phoebe's mood changes. It's almost like she is here to have fun and the auditions just get in the way of that. Her mind is twisted. Since Liam and I are alone for at least a few seconds, I decide to pump him for information. "You and Phoebe are pretty tight, huh?"

"Yeah, it's a sib thing," he says, brushing a few of his bangs off his forehead. A sib thing? Please. You don't see me holding Christine's hand before a big soccer match, and the last thing I need is help from my sister at a go-see.

"Do you always go to auditions with her?" I ask.

"Yep. Mom and Dad don't want her going alone, and Phoebe gets really nervous if she doesn't have me around."

"Really? Phoebe has a bad case of nerves? That can be very difficult to overcome," I say, but realize my tone is much too joyful. So I add, "I understand.

I get really, *really* nervous too." It even sounds funny saying it. The truth is, I have *never* once been nervous for an audition. I grew up doing this. I'm more nervous brushing my teeth than I am at a go-see. Phoebe can't handle the pressure. That must be when she forgets her lines.

"She won't go out on go-sees unless I go with her."

"That's pretty nice of you," I say.

"Are you kidding? I love it. You wouldn't believe how many pretty girls are at these things. All the guys at school are totally jealous." Sure this boy is cute, but his know-it-all personality is truly overbearing. You would really have to be hopelessly boy-crazy to even remotely consider going out with him.

"So where's your sketchbook?" he asks.

"At home," I say. "And I should be getting back myself. Tell Phoebe I said good-bye and tell her to break a leg for me." Little does he know, I mean that last part literally. I begin walking out of the office.

"See you around next week," he says.

I stop and turn around for a brief second. "Or maybe sooner," I say.

Liam Marks has no idea that he is about to help me become me all over again.

CHAPTER 21

After figuring out a plan to get back on top, I am in such a good mood that I decide not to sit on the couch and sulk for the rest of the afternoon. Instead, I sit on the front steps of the house and do some drawing. I figure I deserve to treat myself a bit, and drawing always has a way of taking my mind on vacation. It's late in the afternoon and the heat of the day is finally cooling. The long shadows make interesting shapes that I might be able to recreate with a smoky charcoal or pastel.

I open up my sketchbook and sit down, when I notice Christine behind my dad's SUV bouncing her soccer ball on her knees while listening to something through her headphones. I leave the shadows for another time and decide to do a quick sketch of my older sister in thick, gray pencil.

My pencil moves quickly around the paper as I try to capture the essence of her movement. People always think we are twins because we look so much alike. But when I see Christine, I don't see myself at all—I see this totally different person.

I erase some of the marks around her head on my sketchpad and think about the time when I was six and Christine was seven and we went on an audition together. Up until that point Christine had had absolutely no interest in commercials. We were still at the age when we wanted to do everything together all the time, so I used to beg her to come on auditions with me. "C'mon," I would whine. "They take your picture, tell you to smile, and you get to pretend to be someone totally different." Of course, Christine never had any interest in pretending to be anyone other than who she was and why would she? Even at seven, Christine was the girl all the other girls wanted to be friends with. At the go-see Christine walked in, read the lines, walked out, and said, "Can I go to ballet class now?"

Christine was the one who excelled in anything athletic or social, from team sports to ballet recitals. I was always the girl on the box of this or in a commercial for that. It's strange because, even though we look so much alike, no one ever stopped Christine on the street thinking they knew her. They almost always recognized me. That has always been something that is mine. Sometimes I wonder what my life would be like if it was Christine who was in the car when Judith discovered me. Would I be the captain of the dance team and MVP of the soccer league? Would I be the happy-go-lucky one with a steady stream of friends on two continents, while she struggled to make her dreams come true at casting offices all over the city?

"Ni hao ma?" Christine asks how I'm doing.

"Wo hen hao," I say back in Chinese. I'm fine.

"What are you drawing?" Christine asks, popping her earbuds out of her ears and walking over to me.

"Oh, nothing," I say. "Just messing around." I turn to a blank page in my sketchpad. I don't like anyone to see my drawings until they are finished.

"At least you're finally in a better mood," she says. It's weird how a sister can just know something about you. "Did you book a big spot or something?" she asks.

"Not yet," I say.

"So you got a callback for something good, huh?"

"Not exactly," I say, and this time I can tell

Christine knows something is up so I say, "It's just that I have a plan."

Christine smiles broadly, sits down next to me, and says, "Okay, spill it. I want to hear everything." I take a deep breath in, hold it for just a second, and then exhale before explaining my simple, but marvelous, plan.

CHAPTER 22

I look at my four best friends—Priscilla, Jean, Margaret, and Kate's cousin, Katie Jo—sitting there in the drawer, but none of them seem right for this part. Katie Jo could do the job in a pinch but I think I need something a little different. I know exactly what to wear to snag a callback, but getting a boy to notice me is a totally different thing.

Liam will be turned off by anything too bright and cheery, and anything too trashy will look like I am trying too hard. Since I am on my way to an art class I figure I can't go wrong with distressed denim shorts and a black V-neck shirt. Black says I'm creative and moody, something that I think will appeal to Liam. The whole purpose in taking this art class is to get closer to Liam so Forgetful Phoebe won't have her secret weapon any longer.

On my desk I have the brand-new sketchbook, box of pencils, charcoals, and pastels I have purchased for class. I admit seeing all the brand-new supplies, just waiting to be used, makes me smile. I put everything in my backpack and remind myself that there is only one reason I am taking this art class. If Liam were taking a class in auto repair, I would be shoving a wrench and a can of oil in my backpack right now.

Christine thought my plan was brilliant but deeply flawed. "Brit," she said, while bouncing her soccer ball on her knee, "I think you might just be some kind of evil genius."

I took offense. While clearly my plan is a bit genius, it's not evil. "No one is going to get hurt," I told her. "You don't have to worry about Liam or Phoebe."

"I'm not worried about them," she told me. "See, that's the thing about an evil genius: They are always the ones who wind up getting hurt by their own spectacular, but insane, plan."

Christine saw the potential for a huge disaster and advised me to forget the whole thing and just focus on doing my best at my go-sees, but she doesn't know I have already been doing that since we got back and it hasn't made a bit of difference. This plan might be the only thing that will work and—evil genius or not—I have already started putting things in motion.

Class starts at 9:00 a.m. and I plan to walk in at 9:06 so I can truly make an entrance. It is my experience that entrances are utterly important, no matter what the situation. An entrance sets the tone for an event. It tells everyone in the room you are someone to be watched. By arriving a few minutes late, everyone will already be seated and the instructor will have already started talking and everyone will have to look over at the door to see who is interrupting the class. This will also allow me to use the element of surprise on Liam. Sure, he told me about the class and said I should sign up, but I outright refused on the train.

I peek through the window in the door to the classroom and spot Liam. He has his sketchbook open and is giving the instructor his complete attention. That won't last too long. I flip the back of my hair to give it some extra bounce and push the door of the classroom open.

As I suspected, everyone stops to look at me. I'm used to being looked at so this doesn't bother me at all. I can see out of the corner of my eye that Liam is among those staring at me. I don't acknowledge anyone's stare. "Is this Mr. Snyder's class? I'm so sorry

I'm late. I wasn't sure what room it was in. I'm so sorry," I say with a deep sincerity I'm pretty sure everyone buys.

"There is an empty seat over there," the instructor says. "I was just explaining our first project." I walk quickly to my seat. Everyone has turned back to Mr. Snyder and is listening to him. Everyone except Liam, who is still staring at me. I finally decide to acknowledge him. I turn my head, mouth the word "hello," and wiggle my fingers very matter-of-factly, like I had no idea in the world he was in this class. Then I quickly turn back to focus on the instructor so it looks like the class is the real reason I am here.

"Remember," Mr. Snyder says, "a still life is a collection of shapes. The job of the artist is to make an interpretation. We will all see the same objects, but we might not all see the same shapes. One person's triangle might be another person's circle on top of a rectangle."

I sigh internally.

Still life? Seriously? How many bowls of fruit can a person draw in a lifetime? Clearly I am not in an advanced-level class. At least in Hong Kong there were some interesting fruits, like papayas and guavas. This guy will probably just give us a bowl of apples and grapes from the Stop & Shop. Boring. I am about to ask if we have to do this drawing if we have already done a lot of still lifes, when a kid with glasses raises his hand and asks, "So what are we going to be drawing?"

"I don't know," Mr. Snyder says.

Oh, great. This clown hasn't even brought in his own fruit. Everyone looks a little confused.

"I don't know because I want you to create the still life as a group." He moves his desk to the center of the room and we all make a circle around it with the desks that are set up as artist easels. "I want each of you to put something that you have brought with you on this desk to create the still life. It can be anything you want. It might be something you think is challenging to draw or something you think is fun to draw. It just has to be something that is yours. The challenge is where you put your object and how you make it part of the still life. So grab something and let's get started."

My mind starts going through all the things I have with me that might work. I like a challenge and Mr. Snyder has certainly given me one. I could use some of the things I have in my makeup bag or maybe tear a sheet out of my sketchbook and crumple it up since that would make a very interesting shape.

First a short boy with freckles and small eyes puts some sort of action figure in the center of the room and everyone groans just a bit, since an action figure is just as complex as drawing a human figure. Mr. Snyder responds to the group saying, "Remember, every object is just a series of shapes." Kids continue to add to the still life with art supplies, house keys, and various other objects you would expect kids to have. Then a tall, willowy, blond girl walks to the center of the room empty-handed, leaving the rest of us perplexed by what she might contribute. Then she takes off her shoe and adds it to the growing sculpture. I immediately like her for showing such panache.

When it's my turn, I finally decide to contribute the one thing I always have with me no matter what. I walk to the center of the room and, against the blond girl's shoe, I prop up my headshot. Mr. Snyder looks a little surprised. He probably was not aware he had any professional kids in his little group. "It's my headshot," I say.

"Yes," Mr. Snyder says. "We can see that."

When the still life is finished, Mr. Snyder gives us a few further instructions. He tells us to really "see" each part of the still life and to observe, using the pencil as our eye. I take a few minutes to really look at the still life. It is one of the strangest collections of objects I have ever seen and it includes an eight by ten photograph of me at its center. It is less a still life and more a wacky sculpture, but there is something about it I find very compelling, the inclusion of my image aside.

After really taking in the sculpture with my eyes, I put my charcoal on the paper and begin. I start with the shoe and do my best to really convey on paper what it looks like. Mr. Snyder is walking around the classroom, helping each person with his or her drawing. When he gets closer to me, I get nervous.

"Wow!" he says. "This is great."

"Thanks," I say. "But I am having problems getting the . . ."

"Oh, here?" He points to the exact part where I am having difficulty and takes out the sketchpad he has been using to demonstrate with and begins to draw. "See, if you think of this area as a rectangle and this area as a cone plus a square . . ." His pencil glides over the paper and I suddenly see what he is talking about. I make the adjustments on my own drawing and suddenly everything snaps into place. "That's it," he says. "Exactly."

I smile and keep drawing. Mr. Snyder goes around to work with the rest of the kids. I stay focused on using shapes to see the objects.

"Okay, everyone. Time to pack up. I'll see you at the next session." How is that possible? I look up at the clock in the center of the room and, sure enough, it shows that nearly three-quarters of an hour have passed since I began my drawing. I would have thought I had only been drawing for ten or fifteen minutes. I was completely lost in the assignment. I put my sketchbook flat on the desk and step back to see if there are any parts I might be able to improve. As I am looking at my drawing, I feel someone come up behind me.

"Nice work," Liam says as he walks past me and out the door. "See you around." I get a knot in my stomach when I realize what I have just done. How could I have been so stupid?

The whole point of this class is not to learn how to draw a still life or play with charcoals and pastels. The whole point of this class is to get some face time with Liam and get him to like me. I just wasted one whole class on this stupid drawing when I could have been flirting with Liam.

I am so mad at myself that I take my sketch, fold

it in half, and rip it down the middle. The tear makes a noise so loud Mr. Snyder comes over to see what is going on.

"Hey, what are you doing?" Mr. Snyder asks. "Didn't you like it? I thought it was really good. One of the best in the class."

"It wasn't what I was trying to capture," I tell him, placing my supplies in my bag.

"You know," Mr. Snyder says, putting his hand on his chin, "there are some Native American cultures that believe all art must be destroyed once it has been created so something new can take its place." He gives me a look that shows he is looking for some type of response.

"Well," I say, grabbing my backpack and placing it over my shoulder, "I'm a girl who is all for destruction and replacement. It's just that some things are harder to destroy than others." I walk out of the room more determined than ever.

CHAPTER 23

Sometimes an audition is done in fewer than thirty seconds. You walk in the door, fill out your size card, and look over the copy. The casting director calls you in, you slate, make the copy come alive, and you are out of there. It's rare that an audition goes that quickly, but it happens. My morning audition was like clockwork. I was in and out in under thirty seconds.

My afternoon audition is at Casa Casting near the ultra-cool Meatpacking District. I guess at some point they packed meat in that part of the city, but you would never know it now with all the fancy clothing boutiques and chic outdoor cafés in the area.

Casa Casting fits in the neighborhood well. The office is all steel and glass with windows that look out over the High Line park and the Hudson River. Before you walk into the office, there is a sign listing all of the commercials they are casting that day. Arrows point in the direction of the studio in which each commercial is casting. I scan the list: Snack Its, Target, something that must be a new drug that begins with a "Xeo," and then finally Gravity Gum, the spot I am here for. The arrow points to the studio in the back. I walk down the hall and as soon as I turn the corner, I see dozens of girls waiting to go in. Without hesitating I go right to the sign-in since the sooner I sign in the sooner I'll go in. I grab a copy of the sides and start looking for a place to sit down.

Seven minutes go by. No one has gone into the studio and no one has come out. There have to be at least a dozen girls in front of me so that means I will be stuck here for at least an hour. Luckily, I have brought my sketchbook with me to help pass the time. I scan the room and see if there is anyone specific I should focus on for my drawing. I can't decide if it is good or bad that I don't see Phoebe here. I'm sure she'll show up before I go in.

With Phoebe gone I have a chance to focus on the other girls in the room. Some of the girls are new, but some I have known for years. I guess "know" is not really the right word since I have never really seen them outside of an audition, but in a way we have grown up with one another.

I notice Jess waiting with her mother near the entrance to the studio. I realize I don't really know anything about Jess except for the fact she always wears green to make her shiny brown hair stand out. Jess is not someone who books an amazing amount of stuff, but I have seen her on a few spots and she isn't terrible. Her hair is pulled back off her face, as per industry standards, and she is playing some sort of handheld video game to pass the time. Next to her is a girl in an outfit almost identical to Jess's, with a small variation in color. I think her name is Beth or Betsy or something with a B. She has not been around that much, but she already has The Look. I know The Look because I was born with it, but others need to take time to develop it.

We commercial girls all look the same in some ways. Our hair color may be different and some of us may be taller than others and there are even girls from different ethnic backgrounds, but we all look the same. None of us are dogs, but no one is runway-model pretty either. Judith once told me that to be in commercials you need to look like you could be someone's best friend, and I guess that is what each of us look like, someone's best friend, which is rather odd since very few of us are actually friends with one another.

I flip through some of the pages and realize that all my sketches of the girls I see at auditions remind me of someone. Someone I know very well.

It takes a few seconds and then it finally hits me. All of the girls remind me of, well, me. To confirm my suspicion, I look around the room and put my sketchbook to the side. Everyone looks bored and tired, but I *know* the moment the studio door opens and the camera turns on, each of these girls will light up with enthusiasm, like it's the first day of summer vacation.

Cassie, the girl who booked that Seven Sails spot with me, sits on a stool with her feet dangling. She looks bored, but rumor has it she has a major crush on that kid Rory Roberts. I bet she is waiting to see if he is at a go-see in the other studio. I study Cassie for a second until I realize we are both wearing the same exact shirt. In any other situation this would be considered a social faux pas. Here, it's normal.

The door finally opens and a short guy with spiky hair says, "Sorry everyone! I'm running really late.

Moms, can you make sure your girls have the copy down? And girls, if you are here on your own, can you make sure you know the copy before coming in? It will make everything run much faster." He looks down at his clipboard and then says, "Faith Willis. I need Faith Willis in here."

I know Faith. She even gets her hair cut at the same salon I do. Same stylist, too. She gets up from a chair and goes into the studio. As she does, three more girls enter the waiting area from the hall and go to sign in. The new arrivals fit in perfectly.

Each one is just a slight variation of the other.

Each one is just a drop in the sea of me.

CHAPTER 24

During the next two weeks I do my best at every audition and callback I get. I even book a spot that shoots a few towns away from where I live for a bank. Judith is happy for me to get the booking, but it's only a regional spot and not a national booking so it's more of a consolation prize than first place.

I have banned my family from having any of the TVs in the house on while I am home for fear of seeing Phoebe's face on-screen, but when I come home from my regular workout, my father has the forty-two-inch television blaring in the great room. I try to ignore it and grab a peach out of the bowl on the counter and open the fridge for a cold bottle of water.

I'm still breathing heavily from my jog and I let my lungs fill and empty with air, enjoying the sensation of having completed another workout. Commercial girls don't have to be super thin, but we have to be in shape so it looks like we don't spend all day on the couch playing video games and eating ice-cream sundaes. I screw the cap off the ice-cold bottle of water and begin to take a drink when I hear it.

The jingle for Pizza Fantastic sounds like someone took a bag of Care Bears and put them in a blender with a bottle of maple syrup. It is disgustingly sweet and happy. They draw out the first word like it is a hallelujah chorus and then say the word "fantastic" like they are on a space shuttle. It's so stupid. The only thing worse than hearing the jingle is knowing that I am only a few seconds away from seeing and hearing my least favorite person in the world.

I march into the family room and as soon as my dad sees me, he leaps up from his chair. The look on my face must be intense because he starts searching for the remote and says, "Oh, baby, I didn't know you were home. I was just watching some of the game and . . . ah . . . where is that remote?" He starts looking around his chair and under the cushions, but it is too late.

Phoebe is on a boat, smiling with her family. Her mother is the woman I saw at that audition a few weeks ago and her dad is played by this really funny guy who played a police officer in a commercial I was in a year or so ago. I think his name is Tim or Tom or something. The kid playing her brother is that boy Rory Roberts. Phoebe and her family are fishing off the boat when suddenly her brother pulls up his fishing pole and, instead of a fish on the end, there is a pepperoni Pizza Fantastic pizza on the end. The whole family laughs, and then you see them getting a pizza delivered to their campsite.

It has to be the stupidest commercial in the history of stupid commercials. Who in the world has a pizza delivered to a campsite and who in the world would want to eat a soggy pizza that has been floating around in a lake for who knows how long?

My father suddenly finds the remote and shuts off the TV with a relieved look on his face. "Was that your friend Phoebe?" he asks. It is incredible how parents sometimes know how to say the exact wrong thing at the exact wrong time.

I try to keep a lid on my rage and say slowly and deliberately, "Phoebe. Is. Not. My. Friend." I turn and walk out of the family room and head upstairs.

Phoebe Marks must be stopped.

She is single-handedly ruining my career. My face

gets red and I can feel all my anger and frustration rising up inside me. For a second I think I will let out a scream so loud our neighbors will call the police, but before the scream gets to my throat, I remember I have an art class today. Phoebe had better enjoy the spotlight while she can because her time center stage is about to come to an end.

CHAPTER 25

It's just like any other go-see, I tell myself. I am auditioning for the role of Liam's girlfriend and I just need to treat each art class like a callback for the part.

I open my closet and consider which outfit would be best for the role. Last time my black shirt was too boring. Liam is an artistic guy so anything too preppy or too sporty is out. Something girlie is always good when dealing with a boy, but Liam probably also wants something artsy. I push around a few hangers to see what my options are and then I spot the perfect costume for this role—a pink T-shirt that I ordered from this cool site online. It has a bunch of different pencils and erasers on it fighting with each other. It's definitely an inside joke for anyone who has ever tried to complete a drawing. I fold it and place it on my bed with a pair of blue board shorts that would be too sporty if it weren't for the lime and yellow flowers across the back.

I take a quick shower, make sure my hair is perfect, and put on just a bit of makeup. I dab some shimmering taupe shadow on my lids and give my lips a brush with a gloss a few notches glossier than I might usually wear. I throw on my costume and look at myself in the mirror the way I would before a go-see.

I scrutinize every aspect of my appearance. The image staring back at me looks like it could fit the part. I am almost satisfied with the result but realize I have forgotten my props. I grab my sketchbook and a fat drawing pencil from my desk and hold them in my left arm, to the side of me. Perfect. I look like I am going in for the role of the girlfriend of a know-it-all guy who likes to draw and tell others what to do. This is one part I just have to book.

The thing about boys is you have to play a little hard to get, but you also have to be clear that you are interested. It is a very fine line. Boys like a chase, but they also are scared of looking like a fool. I remind myself of these details as I walk into the classroom. A few kids are chatting and some others are going over drawings in their sketchbooks. Liam has not made it to class yet so I make sure I pick a seat that has an empty chair next to it. That way, when he does show up, he can sit next to me.

At the table in the front of the room Mr. Snyder has a bunch of old cameras set up, the kind that use film and don't have a screen on the back to show you what you are shooting. I wonder what we are going to be doing with them. For a few seconds I imagine myself using the camera to take some very arty pictures, but my daydream is interrupted by the sound of someone sitting in the empty chair next to me. The sound of someone who is NOT Liam.

"Hey," I say, unable to cover up my annoyance.

"Oh . . . is somebody already sitting here?" the short, slightly overweight girl with freckles now sitting next to me asks.

"Well, actually . . ." I say, thinking of an excuse to get her butt out of the chair I have saved for Liam. Then I see Liam enter the classroom. He walks to the other side of the room and takes a seat, making it pointless to kick this girl out of the seat next to me.

"Oh, never mind," I say. The girl looks confused and a little scared but I don't care. I have only one thing on my mind today.

Liam is deep in conversation with the kid next to

him but I suddenly notice that the seat on the other side of him is empty. I need to get myself into that seat somehow. If I just get up and walk over to it I will look too obvious, and everyone will know that I am after Liam. I need a little bait and switch.

"Excuse me, Mr. Snyder, is there time to run to the bathroom?" I ask. He nods his head and I grab my bag and head out of the room. I wait in the hallway for a few minutes since I have no need to use the bathroom at this time. I just needed a convenient excuse to get out of the room so I could re-enter and claim the seat next to Liam.

After a minute or two I walk back into the class-room like it is the first time I have entered it today. I walk over to the seat next to Liam and say, "Okay if I sit here? Doesn't look like there are any other seats." The truth is there are plenty of other seats, but I want it to look like I am sitting here out of necessity, not desire.

"Sure, Brittany." I sit down, feeling satisfied that I am moving closer to my goal. "So what do you think of class? You ready to thank me for making you sign up?" he asks.

"Oh," I say with my best tone of surprise. "Was it you who told me about this class? I couldn't remember.

I thought it was my mother." Technically, not a lie. Best to keep the fact that he is the only reason I am in this class under wraps.

Mr. Snyder shuts the door to the classroom and says, "Looks like everyone is here so let's get started. Has anyone ever seen one of these strange objects before?" He gestures to the cameras on the table and some of the kids giggle at his joke. "There was a time when telephones only existed inside your house, and they didn't come with cameras inside them."

"Imagine that!" one of the kids says sarcastically, playing along with Mr. Snyder's joke.

"Today I am going to ask you to work with some old film cameras. Artists are very visual people and to develop that part of you, I want you to practice using your sight to see the world around you in different ways. These cameras are going to help you do that." All of the kids look pretty excited since I imagine no one has ever been in a real darkroom before to actually develop film. I know I haven't, and I have done a lot of different things.

Mr. Snyder goes on to explain that our assignment today is to create a "found alphabet." We are supposed to find objects or places in town for each letter of the alphabet. He holds up two photographs.

"See? In this photo of the fire hydrant, the long narrow part of it and the two horizontal spouts on each side make it . . ."

"Make it look like the letter T," I say, suddenly understanding the assignment.

"Great, Brittany," Mr. Snyder says, and then holds up another photo. "Does anyone know what letter this is?" The photo shows the side of McKelly's drugstore building downtown. I never noticed it before but the windows on the wall of the building make an almost perfect H, with two long columns and one horizontal row at the middle.

Everyone is getting excited about the assignment and talking about spots in town that might be good to photograph, when Mr. Snyder says, "Now, I don't have enough cameras for each of you so I would like you to work in pairs."

Bingo.

I have got to get Liam to be my partner. Mr. Snyder starts pairing people off by going around the room and just matching each person up with who they are sitting next to. I breathe a sigh of relief since that means I will be paired with Liam and I won't have to push someone out the window or fake a heart attack to do it. Not that I wouldn't do either of those things.

"And let's have you two," Mr. Snyder says, pointing to the kids next to us, "and you two, Brittany and Liam, working together." As soon as Mr. Snyder puts the two of us together, I look at Liam, roll my eyes, and groan a bit, remembering to play hard to get.

"Guess you picked the wrong chair to sit in today," Liam says, teasing me.

"I guess so," I say, dead serious but careful not to seem *too* upset with the situation.

"Come on. It won't be that bad. This sounds like a cool assignment, doesn't it?"

"Yeah, I guess so," I say, this time pretending to be bored by the whole thing. But actually my mind is racing with a dozen places in town that might work for different letters—like the tree by the courthouse that would make a good letter because of the way the branches are spread, or the jungle gym by the elementary school that probably has half the alphabet in it depending on where you stand.

Mr. Snyder takes a few minutes to give us further instructions on the assignment and explains how to use the cameras a bit. Unlike the camera on my cell phone, these cameras have an adjustable focus and something called shutter speed, which controls how much light the camera sees. "Okay," Mr. Snyder says, "grab your cameras and get started."

I walk up to the table and grab one of the cameras. Next to me, Liam has his hands on a camera as well. "Let's use this one," I say, showing him the camera I have selected. It definitely seems like the newest of the bunch and therefore is probably the best.

"Nah," he says, showing me a beat-up one that probably predates the one in my hand by a decade, "I like this one. It has more character."

"Character? Please. It looks like it was used to photograph the bombing of Pearl Harbor," I say, pointing to the scratched exterior and chipped paint on the back. "This one," I say, assuming Liam will surrender.

"Brittany, no," he says. Two words I do not like to hear together. "This one is better. The lens is sharper," he says, looking through the viewfinder. Since there are some groups without cameras and we are holding two, I just decide to give in. "Fine," I say, and take the camera out of his hand and walk out of the classroom, knowing he is only a few steps behind me.

CHAPTER 26

"*That doesn't look anything like an S!*" I repeat for the, like, billionth time.

"Of course it does," Liam says for the billion-and-first time.

Liam insists that the fire escape on the back of one of the buildings will make a great S, while I keep telling him that the broken pipe on the other side of the building is a much better example.

In the hour or so that we have been working together, we have spent more time arguing than anything else. He has got to be the single most infuriating boy on the planet. Why can't Phoebe have a normal brother, the kind that sits home playing video games, the kind you can wrap around your finger with a smile and perfectly-timed flip of the hair? Liam has to be an *artiste* and, worse than that, he has a mind of his own, which I find endlessly irritating. Maybe I should just abandon my plan and go back to one of the others. Shaving Phoebe's head would be a million times easier than getting her brother to date me.

My cell phone vibrates and I go to answer the call. "Can't you let that go to voice mail? We have, like, half the alphabet to do still," he says.

I look down at my phone and see that Judith is calling. I have been on hold for that gum spot for a while. I pray this is the call telling me I booked it.

"It's my agent," I tell him. "This will only be a second." I walk a few feet away for privacy and answer the call.

"Hi, Judith," I say. "What's up?"

"Hi, Brittany. I just called to tell you that you have been released from your hold for the gum spot. I'm sorry. But don't worry, we'll get the next one."

We'll get the next one. That's what Judith always says when I don't book something, and in the past this has been entirely true. But lately I'm wondering if Judith even believes it anymore. What is wrong with me when I can't even book a stupid print ad for some stupid gum?

"Judith, do you happen to know who booked the spot?" I ask as calmly as I possibly can.

"Oh, it doesn't matter," she says. I can tell she knows and just wants to get off the phone.

"It matters to me," I tell her.

"Look, you will make your comeback. You know the end of the summer is when all the really huge campaigns come out. Let's focus on that, okay?"

"I will," I tell her, "but I want to know who booked the gum spot, if you know." I don't want to be pushy but I want to let her know I am serious about wanting to know.

Judith takes a breath in and then sighs and says on the exhale, "Phoebe Marks."

"Thanks, Judith. We'll get the next one," I say and hang up. I've gotten all the information I need. This time, when I say I'll get the next one, I *really* mean it. Forgetful Phoebe can keep her hair and natural skin tone, or whatever it is that lets her book so much; I am going after her secret weapon. I've got her good luck charm standing a few feet away from me. I don't care if he behaves like a know-it-all creep, I'm going to make him like me if even it kills me. Time to kiss my pride good-bye and let Liam lead the way.

I walk back over to Liam and say, "You know, you're right. That fire escape would make an excellent S. Let's take a picture of it and use that."

Liam looks at me strangely. "Are you alright? Was that your doctor on the phone or something?"

"I'm perfectly fine," I say sweetly.

"If you say so, but the Brittany Rush I know does not give up so easily."

"You're right," I say. "She doesn't give up at all. Let's go snap that fire escape." I hand the camera to Liam and walk over to the back of the fire escape where we can get a good picture.

We finish most of the rest of the letters without arguing. Once I decide not to be so difficult with him, I am actually able to enjoy the project more. Why is it that this kid just brings out my most stubborn side?

"Let's grab a slushy or something from Scoops on Oak Street and review what we still need to get," I say.

"Sure," he says. "Why not?"

We walk over to Scoops, where a few other kids from class are also taking a break. I order a lime slushy and Liam orders a blue Hawaiian one, and we go to sit on the bench on the street in front of the store.

For a few minutes we sit in silence and watch people going by. Downtown Great Neck is totally different from Manhattan. None of the buildings are over five stories high and everyone on the street seems to live in the area. I recognize kids from school who I haven't seen in a long time or their parents, brothers, or sisters. Liam and I just sit on the bench under the store's awning, enjoying the shade and the chance to sit down.

"I guess we should go through our list and see what we need to get," Liam says, breaking the silence.

"Sure," I say, taking out a pencil.

We check and cross-check our list and realize the only letter we still have to get is Y. Who would have thought Y would be so difficult?

"Hey, I've got an idea," I tell him. "Let's go to the old movie theater on Main Street, the Revival, and see if there are any movies playing with Y in the title and we can take a picture of that."

"Awesome idea," Liam says. I can't figure out if making him smile makes me feel good because it means I am getting closer to him in order to carry out my plan, or if it just feels good.

Liam carries the camera and we walk down the street, turning right on Main toward the movie theater. As we get closer, we see that *Star Wars* is playing.

"Great," Liam says sarcastically. "Why can't it be *The Yizard of Yoz*?

"Or *Yostbusters*," I say, playing along with the joke.

Then Liam takes his finger and points a few feet in front him and says in a crackly voice, "Or Y. T. phone home."

That bit actually makes me laugh out loud. I never really noticed before, but Liam can be really funny. The truth is, most of the day when we weren't working or fighting, we were laughing.

"Ugh! It shouldn't be that hard to find a Y. It's just a straight line with two other lines sticking out like this." I take both of my arms and extend them out at forty-five-degree angles.

"That's it!" Liam shouts, and my arms drop.

"What's it? Where? Do you see a Y?"

"You," he says, grabbing the camera and looking through the viewfinder.

"We already have a U!" I remind him. "We took a picture of the necklace in the window of the jewelry store. Remember?"

"No not U, YOU!" he says.

Now I am totally confused. "What are you talking about?"

"Put your hands up again," he instructs. "You, Brittany, are our Y."

"Oooooh," I say, finally cutting through the confusion. I throw my hands up in the air and stiffly turn my whole body into the letter Y under the marquee of the movie theater.

"Great. Hold it right there," he says, and snaps a picture.

Our project is complete. However, Liam takes a few more snaps of me with my arms down and my body not in the shape of any letter in particular.

"What are you doing?" I ask.

"Well, there are a few exposures left and I thought I would just use them up."

I've spent most of my life in front of cameras, yet somehow, with Liam behind the camera, I actually feel self-conscious. I flip my hair off my shoulders and try to smile. Usually when I smile in front of a camera, my smile has a purpose—like to show how good the frozen pizza tastes or to explain that I love my new cell phone. The smile I have in front of Liam doesn't have any purpose at all. It's just a smile because I am happy. It feels totally different.

"Great," Liam says. "I think we finished the whole roll."

"And we finished the assignment," I add. "I can't wait to develop these and see how they look."

There is a bit of awkward silence. It's weird how some silences can be totally fine and others feel like someone is pulling your hair out. We are still standing under the marquee at the movie theater, and I know his house is in the other direction down Main toward school and mine is on the other side of the park.

Finally one of us says something.

"Have you ever seen *Star Wars*?" he asks, but he is not asking me in a way that makes me think he is just asking me if I have seen the movie. He is asking me in a way that makes me think this question will lead to another question.

I've seen *Star Wars* at least a dozen times. It's my dad's favorite movie and he has made Christine and me sit through it countless times. According to my mom, in college he had *Star Wars* sheets that she made fun of him for, and he wanted to name Christine Padmé when she was born. Even so, I say, "No, I haven't."

"You haven't seen *Star Wars*?" he asks. "Well you have to. It's an amazing movie. I've seen it twice and it was even better the second time. Let's go see it."

"Together?" I ask. I know it's a stupid question but I have to play a little bit hard to get.

"Yeah. This Friday night. What do you say?"

I pause for a second before giving my response, like I would if I were tasting a new cereal in a commercial. You can't just put the spoon in your mouth and paste a big smile on your face. You need to take just a second, or even half a second, to let the experience register. I do the same thing with Liam and then say, "Sure. See you on Friday."

I turn and walk away, making sure my hair is swinging from side to side. I just got a callback for a part that is going to really open doors for me. When Forgetful Phoebe finds out that I have a date with her brother, she is going to flip. She might not even be able to slate her name at her next audition.

CHAPTER 27

Just my luck. I don't see Phoebe at any of my auditions the rest of the week. Of course, when I want to avoid her, she is everywhere I look—but now, when I want to drop the bomb on her about my upcoming date with Liam, she is nowhere to be found.

The morning before my date I have a callback for Tyler Soups. It's a simple "bite and smile." I just need to go in and pretend I am enjoying the best soup I have ever had. No problem. There are only two other girls in the waiting area when I go to sign in and get my size card. That's good. The fewer the girls the better my chances.

I sit on the bench next to the studio and fantasize about telling Phoebe about my date. She'll say something like, "You can't! He's my brother. You can't go out with my brother! I need him. I need him at my auditions."

Then I'll say something like, "I'm sorry, Phoebe." Of course, I won't mean it and I'll say it in such a way that she will know I don't mean it. That will be key. Then I'll say, "How does it feel to have something you care about stolen from you?" Then I will smile a devious smile that shows I have won and totally destroyed her. And, for good measure, I'll add, "Without your brother here I really hope you don't *forget your lines.*" This part I will say innocently in a breathy, sweet voice, and then I'll say, as harshly and sarcastically as possible, "Good luck with that."

I close my eyes and imagine the scene over and over. I imagine Phoebe getting so upset that she runs out of the studio. She gets to the street and she whips out her cell phone and tells her agent to cancel all of her auditions and bookings. She is quitting the business. A few weeks go by and people ask me if I have seen Phoebe and I just say, "I have no idea where she could be. I did hear she had a total panic attack and is on the verge of a nervous breakdown." Then I catch myself and say, "But really, really, really don't tell anybody. I don't want it to get around that Phoebe is a basket case, even though, you know, she totally is."

This last part of my fantasy is my favorite part. I sit on the bench and go over it a few times with my eyes closed just so I can enjoy every detail.

"I can't believe you would do this!"

My eyes flash open and standing in front of me is none other than Phoebe Marks.

"I can't believe you would do this!" she repeats, only this time her voice is a little louder. Oh, how I wish I had written down some of the choice dialogue from my fantasy so I would be ready for this. I am about to have my big confrontation with Phoebe, so I guess I will just have to improvise some of the parts of my fantasy. I quickly remember my first line.

"I'm sorry, Phoebe." I say, making sure she knows I am not sorry about it at all. Of course, I have forgotten that Phoebe could miss a clue if it was duct-taped to her forehead.

"Well, you had better be," she says, but instead of having an angry, accusatory tone, she actually sounds playful and giddy. Suddenly, I am confused. What's going on here?

"How could you not tell me this awesome news? You should have called me. Instead I had to hear about it from my brother," she says, smiling.

I quickly try to make sense of what she is saying.

"Awesome" in most parts of the known world means something good. Phoebe said she thinks this is *awesome*. So she thinks me going out with her brother is a good thing. I am confused.

"Excuse me?" I say. I really don't know what else to say since my fantasy script is basically useless at this point.

"Don't you play with me! I know all about your date with Liam. I am so excited for you, for the both of you." She claps her hands together like a trained seal. "Liam is the most amazing brother and you are an amazing friend and the two of you together is just, well . . . it's amazing! I am so excited. Have you thought about what you are going to wear? Maybe you should wear something like I wore in that Seven Sails amusement park commercial. I wore that cute pink . . ."

Phoebe keeps on babbling but I am unable to make sense of any of the words coming out of her mouth. I was sure that me stealing her brother from her would make her furious. It would certainly push me over the edge if the situation were reversed, but Phoebe is actually happy we are going out on Friday.

"And you guys should totally go to Scoops. I mean, I know a lot of high-school kids go there, but you guys are on an official date so why shouldn't you go there too, right? And then you should . . ."

Phoebe does not stop babbling, and I am in such a state of shock I am unable to do anything but remain in a state of shock until I hear a woman yell from the door of the studio, "Brittany Rush. I need Brittany Rush in here pronto."

"Ah, Brittany, they are calling you in for the callback," Phoebe says, and gently pokes me on the shoulder.

"Oh," I say, finally breaking from my state of shock. I walk into the studio and I am so confused by the recent chain of events that I am barely able to remember my name.

CHAPTER 28

Sometimes at a callback you go in with a certain idea in your head about how a line should be said. Like when I booked that spot for Toaster Treats. I was supposed to take the toaster treat out of the toaster oven and say, "This is way better than Dad making breakfast." The first time I said it at the callback, I placed the emphasis on "Dad," to convey that when he makes breakfast, it basically stinks. Then the director told me to try it so I convey that Dad's breakfasts are good, but that the toaster things are even better. I did what he said and booked the spot. In the business that's called "making an adjustment."

If I want to get Phoebe out of my way so I can regain my number one spot, I just need to make an adjustment to my plan. Sure, I thought dating her brother would be enough to make her furious and for him to stop showing up at auditions causing her gigantic case of nerves to return and she'd start forgetting her lines. But now I see that, in Phoebe's demented mind, this is a good thing.

What I have to do is go out with him and get him to like me, to really like me, and then once he does I need to break up with him. I'll need to dump him so hard and so publicly he will never show his face at a go-see again, thus putting Phoebe's career on permanent hiatus.

Liam thinks he is some type of artistic prodigy and my little plan has the added bonus of giving him a good dose of reality. As for poor Phoebe, she was never cut out to be booking as many spots as she does. The poor thing is probably exhausted. My plan is just going to make it easier for her to get out of the business, rather than waiting until she crashes and burns. I know on the outside my plan looks less than ideal, but the reality is I am really helping everyone.

I wish Christine were still here. She left for a soccer clinic in Pennsylvania a few days ago, just before my plan got, well, complicated. I know I could call her but part of me is afraid she would convince me to stop the whole thing and that is something I am not willing to do. I have to make this work.

I keep reminding myself of all this as I sit on the edge of my bed wrapped in a towel, about to get ready for my date. There is a part of me that is actually nervous. I think I have butterflies in my stomach and I would bite my nails if I wasn't concerned about them looking chewed on.

I wonder if Liam is nervous too. Probably not. Liam is one of the most confusing kids I have ever met. One second he is this stubborn know-it-all and the next minute he is actually listening to me and almost thoughtful. I guess it's kind of him to help his sister at auditions, and the fact that he makes her less nervous means he must be a pretty nice guy.

One thing about Liam that is not confusing at all is how cute he is. I tried to deny it at first, but the fact is, Liam is one of the cutest boys I have ever met. I meet a lot of cute boys at go-sees and on bookings, but he isn't at all like any of those commercial boys. Liam isn't cookie-cutter cute; he has his own look and style. Like the other day in art class he wore this braided leather bracelet. A boy would never, ever wear a bracelet to a commercial audition because it would be too edgy. At go-sees we try to round off any possible edges. Liam doesn't seem to care about any of that. He always wears these vintage T-shirts and his hair is always a messy mop of soft brown spikes that seem to go in every direction.

I hardly ever wear dresses since they are rarely appropriate for auditions, but I think tonight a dress might make a very appropriate choice. I actually only own a few dresses so my choices are limited. I take out an aqua-blue one with a narrow skirt that I like a lot but is too formal for a movie date. Next to it I see the perfect dress for tonight. It is a simple, white cotton dress with tank-top straps and a broad skirt that has enough fabric to catch the wind if there is any type of a breeze.

I usually wear my hair in a very simple, no-nonsense style since I never want my hair upstaging me on camera. But tonight I decide to let some of the natural curliness stay and I blow dry it so it has a lot of volume and looks like I spent the day at the beach. I even put on a bit more makeup than I usually do and finish the whole look with a shimmering lip gloss.

I close the door to my bathroom so I can see myself in the mirror that hangs on the back. I twist so I can see part of my back in the mirror. I look myself up and down and think, *This is me. The image staring back at me, this very second, is really who I am. This.*

This is me. It's not a huge surprise since I see myself around a lot, but what I realize is I am not looking at the me getting ready for a go-see. I am not looking at the me who is about to go in for a spot to play a daughter doing her homework or a sister having a snack at home or whoever it is they need me to be that day. I am actually looking at me, Brittany Rush, going out on a date. Suddenly my stomach fills with butterflies again.

CHAPTER 29

I go downstairs and pray my parents won't make a big deal about me going out with a boy tonight. I try to downplay the whole date aspect of the evening and say I am meeting my friend Liam to go see a movie, but when they see the way I am dressed, they are suspicious.

"What movie are you going to see, Brit?" my dad asks.

I hesitate to tell him. "Um, *Star Wars*."

"Really?" he says, raising his eyebrows. "If I didn't think I would be intruding, I would invite myself along."

"DAD!" I shout. The very thought of showing up with my father is horrifying.

"Brittany," my mother adds with a soft chuckle.

"He's only kidding. Your father has no intention of going along with you on your date."

"It's not a date," I say. "Well, not exactly." The truth is, I don't know what it is, but a date is only what it is on the surface.

"Well, whatever you call it, have a good time. You know the rules and your curfew. You have your phone with you and it's charged?" my mom asks.

I nod and say good-bye and start walking toward the movie theater downtown. About halfway there the butterflies come back. I stop and shake out my fingers to release any excess energy. I've used this trick at some callbacks, yet tonight it doesn't seem to work.

Why am I nervous? I haven't been on a ton of dates but I've been on a few, so it isn't like I have never done this before. Back in Hong Kong, I even went out on almost half a dozen dates with a boy named Tim whose father worked for the same newspaper as my mom. Tim was a sweet, shy boy who was a year ahead of me at school. He barely spoke when we were together, which was fine with me since I like talking. It was easy spending time with Tim because he seemed to like whatever I liked. If I said I liked a certain song, he said he liked it too. If

I said I liked a certain café in town, he would say he would check it out since it must be good.

My last two dates with Tim ended with a kiss. Tim was a nice boy to get my first kiss from and the kiss itself was nice also. I remember being more excited about the fact that I no longer had to worry about when I would have my first kiss than I was about the kiss. Still, I know I will always remember that kiss even if there were no fireworks, or even a tiny clack of sparks.

Suddenly I realize that, in order to complete my plan, I will have to kiss Liam at some point. The butterflies in my stomach quickly go from fluttering to auditioning for Riverdance. Going to a movie and holding hands is one thing, but kissing takes everything to a whole new level. I guess I haven't really thought my plan through.

All I want, all I have ever wanted, is to get my dreams back on track. For a second I consider turning around and running home. I'll hide in the back yard for a few hours and then walk in the door like nothing ever happened. *Turn around,* I tell myself, but my feet don't listen and just keep walking toward the movie theater.

"Hey, Brittany," a voice says from behind me,

and suddenly my stupid feet have no problem turning around at all. I turn and face Liam.

He looks totally different than he does at go-sees. He has combed his hair so it is flat and smooth. His face looks freshly scrubbed and I can smell the lingering scent of Ivory soap. He has exchanged his usual uniform of vintage T-shirt and cargo shorts for a crisp, white polo shirt sans logo and a pair of seersucker summer pants that have those very thin blue and white stripes on them. Usually Liam's look is artsy and edgy, but tonight he looks like he stepped out of a 1950s movie musical. The transformation is surprising and incredibly attractive.

"Hi, Liam," I say, and smile. My butterflies are still there but they are only waiting in the wings now.

We walk side by side down the last block to the movie theater making small talk. There was a sudden summer storm about an hour ago that lasted only a few minutes, so while it isn't raining now, the street and sidewalk are still damp and the lights from the stores and movie theater marquee reflect and glow on the wet, smooth surfaces. Since it's Friday night there are a bunch of other couples outside the theater who also look like they are on dates. Some of the boys have their arms around the girls. I wonder if Liam will put his arm around me.

After we get our tickets, Liam buys us popcorn, Junior Mints, and a Diet Coke. We decide the seats in the mezzanine will give us the best view so we go up the stairs. The area is almost empty, and we grab seats front and center.

We sit in silence for a second. I know I should be making conversation with him, and usually I don't even think about making conversation with him, but tonight there is an awkward silence. I look around the theater searching for something to say. The Revival sparkles with gold leaf and intricately painted murals. "Hey, look over there," I say, and point to one of the beautifully carved figures that lines the edges of the area around the screen.

"What?" Liam says, looking in the direction I am pointing. At first he is confused and then it dawns on him. "Oh, that would have made a perfect Y! I wish we still had the camera."

"I know," I say, looking over at the figure who is holding up her arms in a perfect Y.

"And over there," Liam says, pointing to another architectural detail that resembles a letter. Soon we are examining the ornate interior together and pointing and laughing and the awkward silence has just melted away. We are so wrapped up in our conversation we barely notice when the lights dim and the movie begins. An older man a few seats away has to actually shush us and this makes us giggle for a second before we begin to focus on the movie.

Star Wars is one of those movies that is easy to get lost in. There is a beautiful princess and a quest to save the world. Of course, I totally relate to Leia's fierce determination and always pay careful attention to how she gets what she wants.

About halfway through the movie, my hand brushes against Liam's arm. It is the smallest amount of contact. If something like this happened on a crowded bus you wouldn't think twice about it, but here, in a darkened movie theater on a Friday night, it is like someone pulled the fire alarm and buckets of water are streaming out of the sprinklers.

For the last forty-five minutes I think of nothing else but how close Liam's arm is to mine, until the last ten minutes of the movie when Liam adjusts in his seat and moves his arm very casually. For a few brief seconds there is no physical contact, but then he casually puts his hand on top of mine. Liam's hand is on top of my hand. We are a few steps away from actually holding hands. I should be nervous or excited or something, but instead I just smile to myself. It feels good to have our hands touching, and the fact that this moves my plan forward doesn't hurt either.

The movie ends and everyone in the theater applauds, including us, so our hands dash out of the dance they had been doing on the armrest. As we get up to leave, Liam turns to me and says, "So what did you think?"

"It's much better on the big screen than on TV," I say.

He looks puzzled. "I thought you said you had never seen it before."

Whoops. I quickly think of something to cover up my fumble. "I mean, I'm glad I saw it here first on the big screen rather than streaming it or something."

"Oh," he says, nodding his head. I almost blew that one. I remind myself how important it is for this date to go well. "You wanna grab some ice cream at Scoops?"

"Sure," I say, and he puts his arm around me as we head down the stairs. Now we are like every other couple in the theater. Well, almost.

It feels like everyone at Scoops was at the movie—

like getting ice cream here after the movie is required or something. I order a chocolate-covered pretzel ice cream and Liam orders a pistachio cone. Even though it is crowded, the bench outside we sat on the other day is empty since another couple has just left.

"What's your favorite part of the movie?" I ask him.

He thinks for a second. "Well, it's hard to pick just one part since the whole thing is really a piece of genius, so I would have to say anything with Han Solo."

"Really?" I ask. I'm surprised.

"Of course," he says. He seems almost offended. "Han Solo is the coolest character in any of the movies. I mean, Han Solo is the one who makes it possible for Luke to blow up the Death Star."

"I guess," I say, and take a lick from my ice cream. I realize a second after the words come out of my mouth that my tone was a little dismissive.

"Who was your favorite character?" he asks, as if I couldn't say anything but Han Solo.

"Princess Leia, obviously."

He rolls his eyes. "You are only saying that because she's a girl. You're a girl and she's a girl and girls always pick the princess as their favorite character."

I will not sit on a bench outside of Scoops and have some boy tell me what "girls always do"! Who does this kid think he is talking to? I decide to lay out a few facts for him.

"First of all, your precious Han Solo admits he was only in it for the money. He's a smuggler," I remind him.

"Sure, in the beginning but—"

I don't let him finish his sentence. "But nothing. Han Solo is a hotheaded show-off. Leia is the real hero. And even Darth Vader said that Leia's resistance to the mind probe was, quote, considerable. And let's not forget that Leia evacuated the rebel base on the ice planet Hoth." Whoops. As soon as the words come out of my mouth I realize what I have done.

"Wait a minute. The ice planet doesn't even show up until the next movie. How did you know that? You said you haven't seen any of the *Star Wars* movies?"

Me and my big mouth. Think fast, Brit. "I . . . um . . ." I stare down at my ice cream which has now melted so much it looks more like lumpy soup. What is wrong with this boy and why does he have to be such a jerk? I hate being challenged like this. I can feel my face get red and hot with anger and frustration.

The thing that is different about real emotions from the emotions you show in a commercial is that the real ones are harder to control and don't always make sense. Not to mention I don't have quite as much experience with the real ones as I do with the ones I act out on camera. My face gets hotter.

"I . . . can't a girl Google before she sees a movie?" I finally say, and throw my hands up in the air. I've had it with this boy. I stand up, toss my ice cream in a nearby trash can, and flip my hair off my shoulder. "I've lost my appetite. See you around." I walk away from Scoops toward my house.

CHAPTER 30

"Okay, so you are on a first date. You are a little nervous at the movie theater, but you both reach for a Nut-tastic candy bar. Okay? You smile and laugh since this is a sign that you like the same things. Okay? Let's go right to tape on this take. Okay?"

The director moves behind the camera and sits on the couch with the other adults in the studio. I wonder if when he talks to adults he uses the word "okay" so much. Even though the director is totally annoying, I wish I had him on my date the other night with Liam. Maybe he would have been able to remind me to stay focused on my intention rather than get so worked up I actually stormed away from Liam and completely derailed my plan. I should have just nodded my head like some silly airhead. Real dates are so much harder when you don't have a director. Okay?

"Oh, wait," the director yells, and jumps back up from the couch. "Maybe if when you reach for the Nut-tastic bar, your hands could touch a little. Okay? We go right to tape."

The assistant behind the camera says, "In three, two . . ." And then he mouths the word "one" and we do as we were just instructed. The moment that camera goes on, I look at the boy standing next to me like I have had a crush on him since I was in kindergarten, even though I just met him a few seconds ago and I'm not exactly sure what his name is. I think maybe it's Marcus or Marvin or something with an M. It doesn't matter what it really is because when the camera is rolling all that matters is what it looks like. It needs to look like we are on our first date, not that we met a few minutes ago when we signed in to the callback. It needs to look like we are at a movie theater buying candy, and not in a cramped production studio with hot lights over us and an old calculator as a prop for a candy bar. It needs to look like we are having fun, and not slightly nervous and a bit confused.

The camera rolls and we do the scene a few times with the director giving us some small adjustments.

Outside the studio, Marcus or Marvin or something with an M turns to me and says, "Hey, you are really good. I loved the way you took his second adjustment and flipped your hair."

"Thanks," I say. "I'm Brittany." We walk through the waiting area toward the elevators.

"I know," he says. "My mom is an agent. You used to be the Berger's Burgers girl. Right? 'I'll have a kid's meal, cause I'm a kid.'" He sticks out his thumb and points to himself the way I did in all of those commercials. It's nice to have someone respect my body of work.

"Yeah, that was me," I say.

"You were awesome in those. I've seen you in a lot of stuff and at some other auditions. I'm Ray. Ray Cameron."

"Hi, Ray," I say. So much for the Marvin or my something-with-an-M theory.

"Well, I gotta meet my mom but we should hang out some time. Facebook me or something."

"Sure," I say, and he heads out the door.

It's only since I have been back that I have been going on go-sees for commercials set during dates or that involve me playing the role of someone's girlfriend. I still go out for the standard daughter/sister/student/friend stuff, but this girlfriend thing is still new territory.

Maybe not all change is terrible.

"I'd stay away from Ray Cameron if I were you," a voice says from behind me. I don't even have to turn around to know that it's Liam. I'm sure Phoebe is not more than a hundred feet away.

"You would, would you?" I say, turning around and folding my arms. I haven't seen Liam since I stormed away from our disaster of a date. I promised myself the next time I saw him I would apologize for being so cranky and act as sweet as pie.

"Yeah," he says. "Ray Cameron and his buddy Rory are both real jerks. They were on my soccer team last year and, between the two of them, they dated, like, a dozen different girls at the same time."

At first I think about turning on the charm and thanking Liam for his advice, but then I realize he must have watched me with Ray and gotten jealous. The way to get to Liam is to start a little competition.

"Oh, I'm sure they aren't that bad," I say. "Ray has actually been really nice to me." I widen my eyes to emphasize my innocence.

"Oh, has he?"

"Yeah," I say, being as coy as possible. "I think he might ask me out for Friday night."

Liam's eyes narrow. I can tell jealousy is the way to get a reaction out of him. "Well, I guess you will just have to tell him you're busy."

"Excuse me? I don't remember hiring you as my personal assistant."

"Ha, ha," he says, rolling his eyes. "Maybe you should. Friday they are showing *The Empire Strikes Back* at the Revival. I'm sure you don't want to miss Leia's big move, or are you not such a fan anymore?"

"Well, maybe if you watch the movie with me, I'll be able to point out some of the finer details of her character you must have missed," I say, making sure my statement sounds like a challenge.

"Fine," he says with his usual snarky tone and crooked grin.

"Fine," I say with my own version of a snarky tone and crooked grin.

"Then it's a date. This Friday. Same place. Same time."

"See you there," I say as if I am annoyed by the whole chain of events. But I walk out of the building feeling a million times better than when I walked in. I may have blown my first audition with Liam, but I know I will book the spot.

CHAPTER 31

I have no auditions and no callbacks on Friday.

Christine is at her soccer clinic until next week and both my parents are working, so I have the day and the house to myself. Most of the morning just zooms by while I draw in my sketchbook, and by the time noon rolls around, I realize I haven't even been downstairs yet. It's a beautiful summer day so I decide to give my drawing a break and sit outside under a tree with a glass of Crystal Light and some magazines. I know my mind will wander, so really the magazines and drink are just decoys to stop me from thinking about my date with Liam in a few hours.

The first time I went out with Liam, I was nervous, but today I don't really feel nervous. It's hard to describe exactly how I'm feeling, but I am definitely thinking about the date. There is actually a part of me that is looking forward to it. Christine and I don't usually talk about boys, at least we haven't in the past, but this is one time when I wish my big sister were around so we could discuss things. Maybe I'll try to send her an e-mail, but it's not the same thing as sitting on her bed and talking.

I turn the page of the magazine and see an ad for a new organic facial mask for girls. Since I have the day off from commercials and I need a distraction, I decide to see if I can get a jar of the mask at the drugstore downtown.

McKelly's Drugs is downtown, across from the movie theater where I will be with Liam in a few hours. As I walk downtown, I almost forget that tonight's date is not a date at all, but a way of getting my career back. But then I decide that is what made the date a total disaster last time. If there is one thing I have learned from auditions it's that you can't fake things. You have to really believe that the cookie you're tasting is the best cookie in the world or that the shampoo you are using makes your hair the shiniest. I was trying to fake it last time and that led to the disaster.

I walk into the drugstore and shiver. The overly air-conditioned environment causes goose bumps on my thighs. It feels good after a short walk in the grueling afternoon sun. I love walking through a drugstore and seeing all of the health and beauty aids lined up neatly, row after row.

This is the drugstore where I first recognized myself on the packaging of a product. I remember going with my mother to pick up some prescription or something and walking down the aisle of baby supplies. I saw a package of Allersan Baby Wipes, dropped my mom's hand, and pointed at the display. "That's me, Mama!" I shouted. I was so loud that Mrs. McKelly, who owns the store, and the pharmacist on duty came over to see what all the commotion was about. They were both so excited to see that the girl on the package was the girl in the store that they brought out a camera and took a picture of me holding the baby wipes with my picture on it.

"Well, hello there, Brittany. It's been a while since we have seen you in the store. How are you and how is your family? How's Christine? I heard Coach White is glad to have her back. I hear she had a wonderful time in Asia. Did you enjoy yourself?" Mrs. McKelly asks. She looks older than I remember her being when I left. Her hair is almost completely gray and her voice has a bit of a tremble in it.

"Hi, Mrs. McKelly," I say, smiling at her. "Hong

Kong was okay. I like being home better."

"Well, as they say, 'There's no place like home.'" She laughs softly. "Let me know if you need any help," she says, and goes back to working on a display of allergy medicine.

I walk to the far back of the store where the cosmetics and beauty aids are kept. I see the display of special lotions and face creams and start looking for the mask I saw advertised in the magazine. I spot the display for the mask, but it looks like they have sold the last one, as all of the spots for the jars are empty. I scan the corners of the display but nothing is hiding. I guess it was a popular product.

"No way! What are you doing here? Are you looking for this mask?" I immediately know who it is. "I hope this wasn't the last one. Here. You take it," Phoebe says, holding out the last jar of the mask.

"That's okay, Phoebe. You buy it," I say.

"I couldn't. Not when you have your big date tonight with Liam," she says.

"Oh," I say with the most innocent voice I can muster. "He told you about that?"

"Yes, he did. I heard the first date was a little rocky but there are definitely sparks. I probably shouldn't tell you this but . . . I think Liam really likes you."

"Really?" I say. At first I am just excited to hear he likes me, and then I realize him liking me means I am that much closer to realizing my plan.

"Yes. At first I was a little worried because, well, you know . . ."

"No. What?" I ask. I really have no idea what she is going to say.

"Well because, you know, sometimes we are up for the same spots and, you know, it is so important for me to have Liam with me at auditions and if anything bad ever happened between the two of you then, well . . ." She trails off.

Part of me wants her to finish that sentence, but the evil genius part knows exactly what she was going to say.

"Well, I wouldn't worry about that," I tell her, but then decide to push a little bit more. "I mean, do you really need Liam at your side for every audi—"

"YES!" she snaps before I can even finish the word "audition." Yikes. "Before Liam started coming with me, I would get so nervous I barely booked anything. I don't know if you know this but . . ." She pauses and looks around the store, as if there might be someone eavesdropping on us. When she is convinced no one is listening, she says in a whisper, "I used to have a problem with nerves and forgetting my lines and stuff at callbacks and go-sees. It was pretty bad."

I put my hand to my chest in a gesture of feigned shock. "Really?" I say. Please. You would have to have been headless not to have known about Forgetful Phoebe. "You have a problem with nerves?" I ask using my shock/surprised tone.

"*Had*," she says firmly. "I HAD a problem. Ever since Liam started coming with me this last year, everything has turned around for me. I haven't forgotten a single word."

"Oh, I see," I say.

"Well, I really hope the two of you have fun on your date, because you are both just great people," she says, and heads out the door.

I stand there in the middle of McKelly's Drugs just shocked. The thing with Phoebe is she didn't say what she said to make me nervous, or put me off my game, or sabotage me. She genuinely wants us to have a good time. She even offered to give me the face mask she came to the drugstore to buy!

For a second I begin to understand why Phoebe books so many spots. In a commercial you often need to act like you are somebody's best friend. The thing with Phoebe is she isn't even pretending at auditions. I think she is just a naturally friendly person.

Leave it to Phoebe to make even *not* liking her more difficult. Ugh.

CHAPTER 32

I show up to the movie theater only a few minutes late. Liam is already there but doesn't see me since he is studying one of the old movie posters they have displayed in front of the theater.

I tap him on the shoulder. When he turns around, I laugh out loud. "Where did you get that?" I ask, pointing at his T-shirt.

"You like it?" he asks, using both hands to gesture to the graphic displayed on the front. There is a clearly identifiable image of Leia, with her trademark side buns, in silhouette and the words "Leia is my homegirl" surrounding the image. It's pretty funny and actually sort of sweet that he would wear it. "I saw it in the East Village on Eighth Street and I knew I had to wear it tonight."

"Hey, bro! Awesome shirt," a random guy a little

older than us says as he walks into the theater.

"Well," I say. "I'm glad to see . . ." I don't finish my sentence. I was going to say something snarky and combative like, "I'm glad to see you finally realized a girl can help save the federation." But instead I say, "You. I'm glad to see you."

This works because Liam puts his arm around me and we walk into the theater together.

Admittedly, *The Empire Strikes Back* is not the best movie of the *Star Wars* franchise. The lack of compelling screen action makes it easy for my mind to wander. About halfway through the movie, Liam's arm reaches across the armrest to hold my hand. I look over at Liam and he just gives me this small, relaxed smile. Most guys would try to make the move look like an accident or get so nervous their hand would shake or immediately bounce off the girl's hand, as if being repelled by an invisible force. Not Liam. He just smiles and keeps watching the movie.

After the movie we head to Scoops as if it is a requirement or something. "I'm really in the mood for a strawberry milk shake," he says. "Wanna split one?"

"I wish, but I can't. I'm allergic to strawberries.

My face breaks out in hives and I wind up looking like a cross between Jabba the Hutt and Strawberry Shortcake."

Liam laughs loudly and then says, "I'm sure you still look as pretty as you always are." His compliment catches me by surprise, but before I can respond or even react, we are at the front of the line. Liam orders an extra-large vanilla shake for us to split, forgoing his desire for strawberry.

The bench we usually sit on outside of Scoops is occupied by a bunch of kids who just finished a T-ball game so we decide to walk across the street to the park, where there are always a few open benches. Even though the sun has set, it is still warm and humid, so the vanilla shake is a welcome distraction from the heat.

We sit in silence for a while and then start talking about art class and drawing and anime and comics. The conversation just keeps going and I'm not even aware of who is talking and who is listening; we are just having this conversation about things that are important to us and laughing. Everything is so perfect it actually begins to feel like we are in a commercial, but there is no sound guy inches away from hitting me in the head with a microphone and no one is about to yell, "Cut!"

This is real life and, for the first time, it seems almost as exciting.

We hear the bells of the church chime and when they finally ring for ten p.m., we realize the night is pretty much over.

"Do you want me to walk you home?" Liam asks.

"No, that's okay. Your house is in the entirely other direction and I don't want you to get in trouble for being out late." The truth is I *wouldn't* mind him walking me home, but I really don't want him to get in trouble.

"Are you sure?" he asks. He turns on the bench so his face is only a foot or so away from mine.

"I'm sure," I say, looking right at him.

"Well then, I guess this is good night," he says softly while still staring right at me.

"I guess so," I say, almost whispering so I don't disturb the romantic tension that is building.

"Brittany," he says, "I had a really good time tonight." He slightly tilts his head to the right and closes his eyes. I try to remember everything I have ever learned about kissing in my entire life.

For a second I blank on the head-tilt thing.

If the boy tilts right, does the girl tilt in the same direction to show interest or the opposite direction for some other reason? I start off tilting in the same direction, but as soon as his lips get closer to mine I remember I need to go in the opposite direction for nose placement. And as soon as I am in the appropriate tilt, it happens.

Liam is kissing me.

I kiss him back softly and quietly and, for a few seconds, there is nothing else in the world. I'm not thinking about go-sees or callbacks or booking or agents or casting directors. For a few seconds there are only the closing moments of a warm summer night, a melting vanilla milk shake, and this boy kissing me.

CHAPTER 33

I'm sitting across the room from Liam. I'm trying to look at him without looking at him. I arrived a little late for art class. I thought about walking in and sitting right next to him but thought that might be a little suffocating. Instead I took a seat a few away from him and gave a big smile as I sat down. He smiled back just as big so I know I made the right choice.

"Today, we are going back to some of the foundations of art and design. We will be using charcoal to do some gesture drawings," Mr. Snyder says as he passes out large pads of watercolor paper.

"Great," I say. I prefer drawing to taking photographs anyway. Looking through a viewfinder is an interesting way of seeing the world, but there is something really magical about having a pencil move across a blank page and being in control of what that page turns into. Knowing you started with nothing and created an image that is entirely your own feels exhilarating.

Mr. Snyder sets up an easel in the front of the room to demonstrate, and explains that we are going to work with portraits, gesture drawings, and land-scapes. He takes a charcoal from the box on his desk and begins drawing a series of lines that increase in darkness across the paper. "Remember the charcoal is not about *fine* detail. It's a big idea tool. The charcoal is about impressions. What you see with your eye is just a small part of what you see."

That phrase really sticks with me for a second. I'm not sure I understand it completely but it's certainly an intriguing notion.

"Let's work with partners today and for the sake of consistency, team up with the person you did your photo assignment with."

I immediately look across the room at Liam and he looks back at me and we both smile at each other. We take a corner of the room near a sunny window to set up our pads and charcoal.

"You won't mind if I draw you with those big buns on each side of your head," he says, teasing me.

"Don't you dare," I warn.

"Choose one person to draw first and after some time, we'll take a break and the other person will draw. There are no rules here except that you can't talk during the project. You are using the charcoal to communicate, not your mouth."

Liam sketches first and turns the page of his large pad to a clean one. Mr. Snyder instructs us to begin, and the first thing I want to do is tell Liam to sketch me from my right side since directors always tell me that is my best side, but I am not allowed to talk. Anyway, Liam has the pad propped up against the table facing away from me so I have no idea what he is drawing.

I'm trying to remain still and smile softly but it feels incredibly strange to have the boy who just kissed you the other night staring at you with a pad and charcoal while you are unable to say a word.

The thing is, I spend so much time being stared at during go-sees that this feels strangely familiar, yet very different. I know what I have to do when a camera is staring at me. I know how to look in the lens and pretend I am talking to my best friend. I know how to flip my hair so a director will think I am being adorable. I know how to pretend to be someone else. Anyone else. This is totally different.

I look over at Liam, wishing I could see the dark lines take shape. Our eyes meet, and in that moment I get this feeling he is really seeing me. He is not just looking at me. He is seeing me, and the difference is the size of the ocean.

On camera I'm being looked at. But here, with this boy in front of me who took me to a movie and kissed me and is now drawing me, I feel as though I'm really being *seen*.

My purse suddenly vibrates. I reach into it and grab my phone. The small screen displays the name Judith. Usually I would run out of the room to answer her call. After all, Judith only calls to tell me about a go-see or a booking. Instead I just shut off my phone, make a mental reminder to call her later, and go back to my pose.

Then, it hits me.

For the first time I can remember, go-sees are not the most important thing in the world to me. For one crazy moment, I consider abandoning my plan altogether. Maybe I should let Phoebe go on all the go-sees she wants and I'll just have more time to sketch and draw and do something that really matters to me. Why break up with Liam just to book some silly car commercial or print ad for a bank? Maybe it's time to let Phoebe, or one of the other girls who has gotten so good at pretending to be me, go and play me, while I focus on just *being* me.

Mr. Snyder tells us to switch roles and I begin to sketch Liam. My charcoal flies over the paper. Marks become lines. Lines become shapes. I'm in control of this image. What *I* do determines how it looks.

I stare at Liam. He has his arms folded in front of his chest for the first drawing. I try to ignore the fact that those arms had been around me just the other night. That he kissed me. I try to focus on the drawing. In any other situation this would be difficult, but when I am connected to drawing, I lose myself in it.

Mr. Snyder finishes the class by having us look out the window to do some landscapes. Within seconds of identifying my subject, I'm back in drawing mode. The world fades away and it's just me, the charcoal, and the paper.

"Excellent work!" Mr. Snyder says as he stands behind me, looking at my drawing. I snap back to reality. "Your sense of line is quite advanced. You should think about taking my advanced after-school art studio in the fall," he says before moving on to the next group.

I smile to myself and keep working. It's nice to

be seen the way Liam sees me, but it's also nice to be recognized by Mr. Snyder.

Liam stops drawing and comes over to me. "Mr. Snyder only asks the best kids into his after-school program," he whispers, since we are not supposed to be talking. "That's amazing."

Liam is truly excited for me. For a second I think he might just kiss me right there in the middle of class, but then Mr. Snyder says, "Find a new place to look and start a new sketch," and Liam goes back to his desk. I turn the page in my sketchbook and start a new drawing.

I see nothing but possibilities.

What if I did take the after-school art studio in the fall? It would mean no more commercials. The end of go-sees and callbacks, five-a.m. call times, bright lights that make sweat drip down my face, and sitting in cramped dressing rooms waiting to be called to set.

It would mean trading one thing I love for something else I love maybe as much. *Maybe more?* But all my confusion and concern falls away as I begin drawing. The charcoal moves over the paper and my eyes start a conversation with my hands that my brain is not allowed to interrupt.

CHAPTER 34

I've walked all the way home, changed clothes, had a snack, and brought some pencils and a pad outside to the back deck to do some more drawing before I remember Judith called while I was in class.

It's amazing how your mind can shut out the rest of the world when you are thinking about a boy. As soon as I realize my faux pas, I put down my pad and go in the house to call Judith back. It's one thing to not care about an audition, but another thing entirely to be unprofessional. I should have called Judith back within ten minutes of her call.

I dial Judith's number, imagining the range of possible humiliations she might be offering me. Either I got released from some ad I didn't even know I was on hold for or she has an audition for me for a car dealership commercial that will run in a sum total of two counties.

Why do I torture myself with these go-sees?

"Hi, Judith," I say, trying to remain upbeat.

"Brit, thank goodness you called me back in time. I need to submit names PRONTO!"

"Sorry, Judith, I was . . ." I am about to think of an excuse when Judith interrupts.

"It doesn't matter. I just need to know your availability. This would involve a multiple location shoot and the contract would be worldwide for one year, possibly longer."

I can barely make sense of what Judith is saying. "Are you talking about a new campaign?" I ask.

"Of course," she says. "Not only a new campaign, Britty, but a campaign for a new chain of spas designed exclusively for teens called Spa-La-La. This is a HUGE campaign. I mean really big. It's not just national, it's international!"

Judith never gets excited about a spot in this way. She is always the model of professionalism, but if I didn't know better, I would swear she is on the verge of jumping up and down in her office.

"Britty, this is a major campaign. Not only would this put your face on magazine ads, posters, billboards, and Web banners, but it would basically be impossible to watch prime-time TV or open a Web browser without seeing one of the many commercials they plan to shoot for this campaign."

"Really?" The word falls out of my mouth, which has dropped open in disbelief.

"And Brit, they are only seeing a small group of girls they hand-selected so things are really looking up. But I need to know if you are free for the first set of bookings for the campaign."

My mind races. This could be it. This could be the campaign that turns everything around for me and puts me back on top. I start to remember the feeling of turning on the TV knowing that I am only a few minutes away from seeing my face appear in some major national commercial. I rip out the page from the pad where I started my drawing and grab a pen from the kitchen counter. I throw the paper with the drawing I started in the garbage and start writing all of the audition information down on a fresh, clean piece of paper.

CHAPTER 35

The audition for Spa-La-La is at Mel Bethany Casting, which is right on Broadway just below the Flatiron building. As I walk toward the office I can actually feel my heart beating inside my chest.

I'm nervous. For the first time, I'm really nervous.

This is a huge audition. Becoming the spokesperson for Spa-La-La means my face is back, not just nationally but internationally as well, since there will be spas in Berlin, Paris, Buenos Aires, and Shanghai. I remind myself to breathe deeply since the camera magnifies even the smallest amount of stress. I must remain calm and relaxed, like I am going to spend a day with friends at a spa. I breathe in and out. In and out.

For a second it works, but once I start walking again my mind starts racing. This audition is huge.

The reality is that the exposure and magnitude of the spot is only part of it. If I can just book this spot without any interference from Phoebe I wouldn't have to follow through on my plan to break up with Liam. He's not such a bad person after all and come to think of it, neither is Phoebe. If I can just book this spot, I can have my cake and eat it too. I'll be back on the top of my game and I won't have to have broken up with Liam or destroyed Phoebe to have done it.

Please, just this once let Phoebe not get called in for this audition. Is that so much to ask? My brain begins to spin. Everything has gotten way too complicated.

I walk into Mel Bethany Casting and I immediately start scanning the room for Phoebe. No sign of her. I go to sign in, and before writing down my name, I scan the list to see if Phoebe has already come and gone. I don't see her name. *Phew.* Maybe she didn't get submitted for this audition. It's possible, I suppose. With Phoebe nowhere in sight, I grab the sides and start practicing my audition.

The scene looks very simple.

I am auditioning for the role of Spa Girl. The sides say Spa Girl is fun, attractive, and high-spirited. No problem there. She takes her beauty regime seriously and only uses the best organic and hypoallergenic products available. Again, no problem. Spa Girl loves being with her friends more than anything else in the world. Well, that part I can fake.

The sides show Spa Girl with Friend #1 and Friend #2 in plush robes, sitting together at the spa as they receive different types of treatments. Friend #1 is getting a facial, Friend #2 is getting her hair shampooed, and Spa Girl is choosing the color for her manicure. She spots the perfect color and shows it to her friends. "What do you think of this? It's called Boy Magnet." The two friends giggle and nod. The commercial then cuts to Spa Girl walking down a city street with her two friends behind. A crowd of cute boys begins to follow her and Spa Girl waves her brightly painted fingernails at her friends and says, "Looks like it works." They all giggle some more.

It's a cute spot. It has a lot of personality but it also requires perfect timing. Spa Girl has to flash her nails and then wait a beat before saying the last line in the second scene or else the whole thing will fall flat. I can see why they only wanted to bring in experienced girls for this.

I look around the room and I recognize a few of the girls from different spots and a few of them recognize me. There are also a few girls who look like they are total newbies and I imagine they are only here for either Friend #1 or Friend #2 since those roles don't involve any talking.

As I sit and wait to be called in, I realize I'm not as nervous as I was when I was walking here. Once I am actually in the room and in front of the camera, I know I'll be calm; the actual audition always makes me more excited than nervous.

"I'll see Brittany Rush for Spa Girl and Nadia Hope and Kaitlin Feder as the friends now."

I take one last deep breath and walk into the studio. The three of us stand in front of the camera. I can tell the other two girls are nervous as they fidget and look around the studio while we wait for the casting director to adjust the camera. I remain completely focused. Being *in* the studio gives me confidence.

We each slate by looking into the camera and saying our name and agency.

"We're really pressed for time, girls, so we aren't going to do a rehearsal. We are going to go right to tape. Is that all right?" the casting director asks. Without waiting for an answer, she says, "Great. Well the thing here is high energy and excitement, but very natural. This is only the first of many spots so the director wants to see that you can go the distance.

Okay. Let's get this on tape. In three, two . . ." She then mouths the word "one" and I start my lines.

I exude energy and excitement throughout. When it comes time to deliver my last line, I make sure my timing is dead-on. One of the girls auditioning for the friend role actually laughs out loud instead of giggling and when we finish, the casting director says, "Great job, girls—and Brittany—are you sure your agent has cleared you for the book dates? This shoots very quickly."

"Yes," I say, "I'm clear." It's always a good sign when they ask if you are clear, but I try not to show any reaction and play it cool.

We walk out of the studio and both girls tell me what a good job I did. I thank them for the compliments but I am more focused on seeing if Phoebe has shown up. I don't see her anywhere. I could actually book this major spot without any interference from Phoebe. Maybe things are finally looking up.

CHAPTER 36

After my audition, I walk back up Broadway. I go over every second the camera was on. Did I smile too much? Not enough? Did it seem natural? Did I pick up my cues? Was my hair perfect? A hundred questions flash through my brain as I try to recall every detail of my audition. I remind myself to think good thoughts.

I will get a callback. I will book this spot. Brittany Rush is Spa Girl. Period. End of story.

I repeat this mantra over and over again as I walk toward the sushi place in Little Korea where I am meeting my mother for lunch. She insisted we have lunch since I've been taking the train in by myself so much. I think she just wants to make sure I am alive.

When I walk into the crowded restaurant my mom is already sitting at a table, talking on her cell phone, of course. "Hi, Mom," I mouth, so as not to disturb her conversation, and slide into the booth seat across from her.

She ends her call and says, "I am turning this thing off and putting it in my purse."

I smile meekly—*I* have already taken my phone out of my bag and placed it on the table. I know I just left the audition, but when a shooting schedule is tight, sometimes the callback call happens very quickly, within hours even. Luckily, my mom doesn't even notice the fact that I have my cell phone open on the table as she orders the usual sushi combo for us to split.

"Do you know what time Christine comes back from her soccer clinic in Pennsylvania?" I ask, attempting to pry my mind away from the callback.

"I think the team bus pulls into town this afternoon so she should be home for dinner. Oh, so how was your audition?" my mom asks, pulling the conversation right back to where I didn't want it to go.

"Grea—" I start and then reconsider. I don't want to jinx myself by telling my mom it was great so I just say, "Fine. It was fine. We'll see." I pretend it's the least important thing in the world even though it is the exact opposite.

"Well, I'm glad you aren't taking this all too

seriously anymore. Have fun with it! Otherwise what's the point?"

I smile and nod. My mom has never understood how important all of this is to me. She thinks commercials are just a hobby or something I do to make money. I earned enough to pay for the college of my choosing before I was out of diapers. I don't care about the money and a hobby is something you do in your spare time, like knitting or stamp collecting.

The sushi arrives and we unwrap our chopsticks and dig in. I happen to love California rolls so my mom moves all of those pieces over to my side of the table. I place each piece in my mouth while trying to maintain a conversation with my mother and keep an eye on my cell phone just in case Judith calls with a callback.

After lunch I walk to Penn Station to grab the 1:23 train back home. There is no cell phone reception on the underground platform where the train boards so I stay upstairs in the waiting area in case there is a chance Judith calls. I wait staring at the postage-stamp-size screen on my cell phone, willing it to ring.

People rush past me and down the stairs to catch the train, but I wait until the very last second before snapping shut my phone and running down the stairs. The conductor yells, "All aboard," just as I step on the train.

The train shoots out the tunnel and the urban landscape performs its usual fade to suburban green. During the train ride I stare at my phone like I am watching a particularly gripping episode of my favorite TV show. I turn the phone on and off a few times just to make sure it is working properly.

About twenty minutes into the trip, I decide I need to focus on something else or my brain will explode. I go to get my sketchpad out of my bag when my cell phone rings. I open it up to see the number.

It's Judith.

"Please tell me I got a callback, Judith. Please." I don't need to pretend to be cool and aloof with Judith. She knows how important this is to me.

"You got a callback. They want to see you again tomorrow morning."

"YES!" I scream so loud that a few of the people on the train turn to see what the commotion is. I take down all of the information and thank Judith for getting me the go-see.

I did it. I got a callback and I didn't have to break up with Liam to do it. I can't wait to tell him about my callback. I thought I was going to have to destroy my relationship with Liam to book this part. I mean, that was the whole point of getting close to him.

Wasn't it?

I mean, that's why I started to pretend to get close to him, and then I actually got close to him, and then I actually got so close to him that our lips were touching, and then. . . . My mind just trails off. Is it any wonder I love being in commercials so much? They start and finish with the same simple message and are over in thirty seconds. My messy, out-of-control life could take a few lessons from commercials.

The train stops in Great Neck and I am so full of energy I think I could run the entire ten blocks home. I can't wait to tell Christine that I averted a MAJOR crisis.

The train doors open and I start walking out of the station toward home when I hear, "Brittany. Hey, over here."

I turn and see Liam. I am still so pumped that I run over to him and give him a big hug. The fact that I don't see his sister anywhere in sight makes me even more excited.

"What's that for?" he asks.

"I just got some good news. Actually some really great news," I tell him about the callback as we walk through the station together.

"Now what's your news?"

"I saw Mr. Snyder at this art supply store yesterday and he asked me to be in his advanced studio course this fall. You and I will get to see each other after school this year!"

"That's great!" I say. I can't believe how well everything is working out. If I can just stay on track and book this spot, I can have my comeback and keep Liam.

"What were you doing in the city by yourself?" I ask.

"Ah . . . I wasn't by myself," he says with a sort of sheepish look on his face. I think he is going to tell me he was with some other girl, but then we turn the corner and I see Phoebe with her cell phone up to one ear and her hand covering her other ear so she can hear.

How is it possible to go from walking on air to beating your head against a brick wall in under a second?

I know who Phoebe is on the phone with. I even know what she is talking about. She must have had her audition after me, while I was having lunch with my mom.

Phoebe finishes her call and runs over to Liam and me. "Guess what?" she shrieks. "I got a callback for the Spa-La-La campaign!" She hugs Liam and jumps up and down a bit. Liam just looks at me from over Phoebe's shoulder. He doesn't know what to say. I don't know what to say.

For a second I consider just congratulating Phoebe. Let things just happen as they happen. Why not? I think I have finally come to the conclusion that Phoebe just books because she deserves it. Then I think about turning on the TV in a few weeks and seeing Phoebe as Spa Girl and I get this dull ache in my stomach. I have no idea what to do but I know I can't decide in this moment.

I need to go home and think.

I quickly start walking away from them and shout back, "I gotta go. See you guys later."

I am out the station and a few blocks down the road before I'm sure they even realize I have fled. I've got some major planning to do and not that much time to do it in.

CHAPTER 37

I agonize over my decision for the rest of the afternoon.

My first reaction is to do nothing. Just prepare for the callback, keep seeing Liam, and whatever happens, happens. I keep telling myself this is the normal thing to do.

If Phoebe wasn't at the audition, or if she didn't get a callback, it would be a different story. I'd just go with the flow and rely on my talent and experience to get me the booking.

But I have to be realistic here.

Phoebe has stolen every major booking from me since I have gotten back. I haven't seen myself on TV since the beginning of the summer and—more importantly—neither has anyone else. I convince myself that am I being *overly dramatic* when I tell myself that if I don't book this spot, life as I know it will end.

Still, I need to be practical and consider every possible angle.

If I break up with Liam this afternoon then there is no way he will be able to face me at the callback tomorrow. He'll have to make Phoebe go on her own and that might just be enough to throw her off her game and give me an edge. She'll forget her lines for sure and the natural pecking order will return.

It's a terrible thing to do. Of course Liam will hate me, but Phoebe will hate me also. I never thought that would matter to me but I can't help worrying over this small detail. At the beginning of the summer I would have leapt at the chance to destroy both of them, but now I'm not so sure it's all that easy.

When I think about my life, I think of it in terms of thirty-second spots. Most kids think, "Oh yeah that happened when I was five, or, we went on that trip when I was seven." I think of *my life* in terms of the spots I booked. I lost my first tooth right before the Hi-Ho Cereal campaign. I learned to ride a bike on the set of the Trusted Insurance commercial.

We are talking about *my life* here. Do I really even

have a choice? If I want to book this commercial, I have to break up with Liam today.

I text Liam and tell him to meet me at the bench outside of Scoops in thirty minutes. Within a few seconds he texts me back and my plan is set in motion. Now I just have to make a final decision about what that is exactly.

I go upstairs to my room and see that Christine's door is open. She must be home early from her soccer camp in Pennsylvania.

"Hey, how was the soccer clinic?" I ask, trying to cover up the anguish my face must be showing.

"Hey, Brit," she says, and walks over and hugs me. "It was awesome. We had such a good time." She takes some of the soccer jerseys out of her backpack and starts putting them in drawers. "There were girls there from all over the country and we just, like, played soccer and hung out in the morning and then had matches in the afternoon. It was amazing."

"That's great. You must have won a lot of the matches."

Christine laughs. "Actually, we lost almost all of them, I think. But I met some amazing girls who I'm sure I'll see again." Christine puts some more clothes away but then stops and really looks at me. "Is everything okay? You look kind of upset."

"Upset? Actually, I'm totally thrilled. I just got a callback for this major campaign."

"That's great," she says, closing the drawer of her dresser. "But you still look upset."

"Well . . ." I start. I'm not sure I want to tell Christine everything and I'm not sure why.

When she was away, I was desperate for her advice. But now with everything so complicated and the plan all set in motion, it's hard to find the courage. Still, maybe talking with Christine will make me feel better about my decision.

"It's just that . . . well . . ." I pause for a second. I'm still not sure *what* I am going to do. But I decide to see if I can test out an idea on Christine. "I'm going to Scoops in a few minutes." I look out the window and sigh heavily like I'm bored. "I'm going to break up with Liam," I say as if I have just announced I'm going to take out the recycling.

"*What?*" Christine almost shouts, which is quite a surprise since she usually reserves outbursts of emotion for the playing field. "But I thought from your e-mails that you liked him. I mean, I thought you *really* liked him."

I suddenly remember a slightly gushy e-mail I sent her after a particularly fun art class. I guess I was confused then. Or am I confused now?

"I do," I tell her. "I mean I did. I mean . . . breaking up with Liam is just something I have to do to get what I really want." The rationalization sounds totally logical when I say it out loud.

I explain to Christine everything that happened while she was gone. I don't leave out any details.

After I finish explaining everything, Christine looks at me very carefully and then says, "Britty, you *are* kidding, right?" Her words are quiet and calm which makes them all the more serious. "You are actually going to break up with a boy you like just so you can wear some fancy outfit and get your hair done on some stupid *commercial*?"

"Christine!" I shout at her. How dare she say something like that to me? How dare she think me so shallow? How dare she call something I love stupid?

She obviously has no idea what it was like for me all summer, being passed over for Liam's sister. I don't know if she has gone too far or if I just don't want to hear any more. "I actually didn't know what I was going to do, but you just made my decision *a lot* easier!" I turn away from her and go to walk out of the room but turn back before reaching the door. "You'd break up with Liam in a second if you thought staying with him meant never playing soccer again." I pull open the door, and slam it behind me.

I storm down the stairs and away from her room.

Who does she think she is? As if I care about the clothes or the makeup. I couldn't care less about those things!

Christine doesn't understand what it's like to be famous. She's *always* had sports and friends. How easy would it be for Christine if she just woke up one morning and she wasn't allowed to kick another soccer ball? What if all the athletic awards she has won over the years were not only taken from her, but the promise of any more coming to her was obliterated?

It's easy for her to be herself because she knows who she is. She grew up being Christine, while I grew up playing someone on TV who looks a lot like me.

CHAPTER 38

As I walk downtown, I am still furious about what Christine said to me but I have to just wipe it out of my mind and prepare for my meeting with Liam, the way I did for my audition earlier this morning. I'm still not even sure if breaking up with Liam is the right decision, but my fight with Christine made me feel backed into a corner and this is the only way I can see myself getting out.

I need complete focus. I remind myself that I am playing a part. I simply need to show up and say my lines: "Liam, we need to talk. It's not you, it's me." Like a mantra, I keep repeating to myself, *You can do this. You can do this.* If this is the right decision, why is it so hard to do?

When I turn the corner Liam is already on the bench, waiting for me. He smiles when he sees me and I realize I need to not make eye contact with him if I am going to do this. "What's up?" he asks. "What did you want to talk about?"

I keep my eyes firmly on the ground. If I look at him I know I will change my mind. "Liam," I say, and then freeze. Why can't I get these words out of my mouth? Like a Band-Aid that needs to be ripped off in one quick movement, I need to just say what I need to say.

"Liam, I don't think," I start to say as quickly as I can, but before I can finish my sentence, I can feel Liam looking over my shoulder. I finally look up at him and his face shows confusion and concern.

I turn to see what has caught his attention, and coming at us faster than a speeding bullet is Phoebe. "Brittany, Brittany," she calls from across the street. She is panting like she ran the entire way here. Did she figure out my plan and come here to ruin it?

"Liam," I say, "I really need to talk to you."

But before he can respond or even register what I have said, Phoebe has crossed the street and sprinted to our bench.

"I'm so glad Liam told me he was meeting you here." Phoebe is panting as she speaks.

"Take a second to catch your breath," Liam says, being the kind, supportive brother that he is.

Phoebe takes a deep breath and then turns to me. "I just wanted to find you guys to tell Brittany that there are *new* sides for tomorrow."

"What?" I say.

"My agent just e-mailed me pages and pages of script they want to see tomorrow at the callback. It's, like, two and a half dozen pages of text about the spa for a promotional video or something, but they want all of the girls off book for the callback."

"Oh my God," I say. This happens sometimes, but usually they give you a few days to memorize that much copy.

"I wanted you to know since we only have until tomorrow morning. You need to go home and check your e-mail."

"Oh my God," I say again. I don't know what I am more shocked by, the fact that there is more copy for the callback tomorrow or the fact that Phoebe just ran all the way downtown to tell me about it. Why would she do that? "Liam, I've got to go home. I've got to work on this copy." I get up and start walking away from them toward my house.

"See you tomorrow, Brit," Phoebe yells and then Liam adds, "Yeah, see you tomorrow."

I guess I just blew my chances of getting rid of

the competition, but with pages of copy to memorize before the callback tomorrow, I realize if I can't deliver the lines there's no chance I will book the spot. I just hope I've made the right decision.

CHAPTER 39

I did my absolute best at the callback.

I looked perfect.

My lines were perfect.

My timing was perfect. There is nothing else I can do. Phoebe was one of four other girls at the callback so I have a one in five chance of booking this spot.

After the callback I go home and try to remain calm even though the anxiety and pressure is making me crazy. I still can't face Christine or bear to have my parents ask me how it went. I decide to go home and use my favorite bath salts for a long, relaxing soak in the tub.

I walk upstairs to the bathroom with my phone in my hand and suddenly I feel it vibrate. I sit down on one of the steps and take a deep breath.

It's Judith.

This is it.

This is the call.

"Hello?" I say.

"Hi, Brit. I have some news."

CHAPTER 40

You would think I would be happy about being in a major campaign. You would think I would be delighted to have a call time at Silvercup Studios. You would think I would be thrilled to be arriving on set.

Well, you would be wrong.

When Judith told me I had booked the friend role and not the Spa Girl lead, I didn't immediately cry. I took down all of the booking information and thanked her for her help. She told me that regardless of the role the Spa-La-La spot was a huge promotion. I agreed and thanked her again.

I hung up the phone, walked a few steps to my bedroom, quietly closed the door behind me, and then collapsed on my bed into a puddle of tears. All I remember is it was late afternoon when I got the call, and when I finally emerged from my bedroom, my parents and Christine had already finished dinner. I ate leftover spaghetti alone in the kitchen.

My career is over and, since basically my career is my life, it doesn't take a mathlete to figure out I've got problems.

Christine heard me crying and came into my room that night. She thought I was still upset over the fight we had. I explained how I didn't book the lead and we both apologized. I hugged her and, just like that, our fight was over.

She lay next to me on my bed for a while and for the most part we didn't even talk, but at one point she said to me, "Brittany, you are so much more than just the thirty seconds in between TV shows. Commercials aren't life. They're what interrupts life."

I didn't say anything in response. We both just kept staring up at the ceiling, but for the first time, I think I actually heard what she was saying.

CHAPTER 41

My dad turns off the highway into the industrial area of Long Island City where most of the film and television production studios are located.

When I was little, I used to think this was like a secret city. All of the buildings are these massive, gray brick and cement dinosaurs that are surrounded and protected by elevated highways and ramps. Millions of people pass them every day on their way into the city without realizing what magic waits inside these warehouses.

Once you are granted access to the interior, you are transported to any number of locations from tropical beaches to suburban dining rooms. Half the national network commercials on the air are filmed on sets in one of these studios. I thought I would arrive here today like a queen returning from exile. Instead I am just me and, it turns out, I am not even sure who that is.

"You okay, kiddo?" my dad asks as he drives through the maze of surface streets around the studios.

"I'm fine, Dad," I say, but I know he can tell my mood is anything but.

He drops me off at the front door of the building and tells me he'll stay late at work so he can pick me up when I'm done.

I walk into the building and check in with the person in charge of minors, who happens to be a perfectly nice production assistant named Martin. Martin gives me the shooting schedule, shows me where my dressing room is, and points out the locations of makeup, wardrobe, and craft services.

"We are really, really pressed for time today so I need you to drop off your things in your dressing room and then head over to makeup and then wardrobe right away, okay?"

"Sure," I say, with as big a smile as I can muster, and walk toward my dressing room. I have to remind myself there are girls who would tear off their earrings just to step inside a working television studio. Here I am about to shoot not just a national campaign but also an *international* campaign and I feel like I am about to take a pop quiz in algebra.

For a split second I consider turning around, walking out of the studio, and calling my dad to have him pick me up and drive me home so I can go to the final art class this afternoon. Then I remember how strangely I acted with Liam yesterday—running out on him and not returning any of his many calls. He probably thinks I'm a freak and never wants to see me again. I can't really blame him. I almost *feel* like a freak. I don't feel right here and not wanted there, or, is it the other way around? There is nothing I can do about any of it now.

I pass through the first soundstage we will be working on. It's a perfect replica of a city street that could be anywhere in the world. It's urban and gray, but punctuated with bright colorful signs with images instead of words, so the commercial can play around the world I suppose. It's the most perfectly realistic set you could ever imagine, but when you look at it, really look at it, you realize there's nothing perfect or realistic about it.

Just like me.

I walk down the hall on the other side of the studio and past a door with the name Phoebe Marks written on a piece of tape and the words "Spa Girl" underneath it. I know Phoebe is on the other side of that door.

A few doors away from Phoebe is my dressing room. It has my name on it and the words "Friend #1" then the name Deni Akon and the words "Friend #2." *At least my name is on top*, I think. I open the door and a girl about my age with straight, very dark hair is taking a few things out of her bag.

"Hello," I say in an even tone.

"I *can't* believe it," she says. "Brittany Rush is you. I mean, you are Brittany Rush."

"Do I know you?" I ask. I meet so many girls who look like her or look like me I can't really keep track.

"No. But I know you. I mean, I feel like I know you. You were on, like, every drink box I ever drank back home." Finally the recognition I want and deserve, but it doesn't ignite a spark in any way. Then I remember the last time I felt that spark—I was drawing.

"Deni," I say. "You're Deni, right?"

"How did you know that?" Deni's eyes open wide and she looks genuinely shocked.

"It's on the door," I remind her and gesture toward her name.

"Oh, right." Deni is a pretty girl with a small nose and elegant face with dark oval eyes. Her skin is a light caramel color and she has a wide, open smile. I put my bag down at the second makeup mirror in the room and the speaker in the dressing room starts to crackle.

"I need Friend One and Friend Two in makeup and Spa Girl on set for blocking and light." Hearing the phrase over the internal intercom system makes it sound like I have been cast in some demented Dr. Seuss book.

"I hope I can remember where Martin told me makeup is," Deni says.

"I know where it is. We better get going," I say.

Deni and I walk to the other side of the building where makeup and wardrobe operate. We pass production assistants frantically going over lists on clipboards, sound crew testing microphones, lighting crew moving equipment, and camera crew cleaning lenses. It's all rather ho-hum to me but I can tell Deni is new enough to be awed by the spectacle of it all. For Deni, everything is magic and a promise. For me, it's a memory and a bucket of cold water in the face.

I sit in the makeup chair like a zombie in a coma. I stare straight ahead at myself in the mirror as a very nice makeup artist I have never worked with before transforms me from the Brittany I walked in as to the Brittany I used to know from magazine ads and television commercials. As soon as this me appears in the mirror, I recognize her right away, but she's like an old friend you knew years ago but don't have anything in common with any more.

The minute they are finished with us in makeup, Martin shows up to make sure we scuttle off to wardrobe.

My trance breaks when we get to the fitting room and I see my old pal Doris. Her usually pert beehive looks like it has lost a few bees. She is sitting at a table fighting with a sewing machine. It looks like she is losing. "Hi, girls," she says. "Deni, I'm Doris and your first one is over there. Brit, darling, I think I still need to hem yours. One thing I am sure of is I am losing my mind today."

"Where is Channing?" I ask. Usually Doris and Channing come as a set.

"Good question," Doris says without pausing in her battle with the sewing machine. "Mr. I-can't-let-my-tan-fade is on some cruise in South America. Bolivia or something."

"Bolivia is landlocked," Deni says.

Doris stops battling with the sewing machine for a second, looks up at Deni, and says, "Thank you, dear," and then, without missing a beat, goes back to the sewing machine.

The fitting room has clothes everywhere. There are sweaters and skirts and jeans and polos and shorts and dresses. "The director keeps changing his mind about the color palette but only after I have finished hemming everything," Doris finally says when she gets up from the sewing machine. "Right now he wants you girls in shades of green." Doris goes to the clothes rack and pulls an outfit with Deni's name on it and one with my name on it. "Please try these on for now. I got your sizes from your size card, so as long as those are accurate this should all fit."

Deni and I change into our costumes. Mine is a pair of black tights with a black pleated skirt and a pale-green cotton sweater. It's cute. Deni is also wearing a green top, but hers is more teal-green with blue-green stripes and her skirt is denim. The rich colors look good against her dark skin. As soon as I come out from behind the dressing curtain, Doris says, "You both look great. Brit, that is perfect on you. Deni, that looks great, but the skirt is too long."

Deni looks down at her skirt and Doris shakes her head. "I am going to have to do a quick hem with you in it. Brit, you are all done."

Someone knocks on the door and then pops their head in. "Hey, Darlene, they need that wardrobe change for Spa Girl, like, immediately," the talking head says, and then closes the door and quickly disappears.

"It's DORIS!" Doris shouts at the closed door, knowing that the talking head is already on to the next crisis. "Darlene? See. That's what happens when you try to do a shoot that should take two weeks in two days. How am I supposed to deliver costumes to the other side of the studio and at the same time?"

"My dressing room is over there," I say. "I can drop it off for you."

"That would be great, Brit," Doris says, and goes over to a rack of clothes, pulls off a few of the hangers with labels, sticks them in a garment bag, and hands them to me.

"See you on set," I say. I walk out of wardrobe carrying the garment bag and run smack-dab into someone I thought I would never, *ever* see again.

CHAPTER 42

"*Brit-tan-knee!*" she says in her upper-class British accent, and then adds, "*Ni hao ma?*"

I take a few steps back to settle myself after the collision but realize she's asking me how I am in Chinese so I answer, "*Wo hen hao. Ni ne?*" The Chinese just kicks in. I didn't learn a lot of Chinese in Hong Kong, but enough to get around town. When you live in a place for a year that just happens.

"*Wo hen hao,*" Mrs. Wong answers, telling me she is fine. "What in the world are you doing here?" she asks back in her perfect British accent.

"I live here," I say. "Well, not here in the studio but in Long Island. In a house." I'm not making too much sense so maybe the impact from the collision was stronger than I thought. Mostly, I think I'm just in shock. "I'm playing the friend in the booking today, for the spa commercial," I add, hoping I'm making more sense.

The last time I saw Mrs. Wong was at her son Henry's birthday party back in Hong Kong at Club Liquid. I remember she was a *very* elegant and *very* rich woman who chatted with me for a bit while I watched the other kids enjoying themselves, playing in the ocean of balloons. She is an incredibly dignified woman who was always dressed like she just stepped out of the boardroom. Today is no exception. She is wearing a bright red suit with a thin pencil skirt that has elegant black-trim details. Her luxurious black hair is swept up off her face in a tight French twist, and her skin is absolute perfection.

"Mrs. Wong?" I ask. "What are you doing here?"

"Well, darling, don't you know? We own the rights to all the teen spas opening across Asia. It's one of our biggest launches ever." Suddenly I remember something about the fact that the Wong family owns some line of cosmetics that has basically dominated the entire Asian market for decades. Thus her perfect skin.

Now it's all beginning to make sense.

"I wasn't going to fly in until later in the week," she adds, taking her compact out of her purse and using the mirror to examine her lipstick. "But they have decided that the Asian markets are going to launch first so they need to do some last-minute script changes and . . ." She pauses, looks both ways down the hall, and then says in a very loud stage whisper, "I hear it is *not* going well. I'm here to get things back on track." With that, she snaps shut her compact and turns on her heel. "We'll catch up after I clean up this mess! It's so nice to see you. Henry will be so surprised." Her heels click down the hall as she heads toward the set.

My brain is operating at full speed. If I had had more time I would have done a bit of Googling on the spas and found out about this connection, but that just wasn't possible with how fast everything went. Then I begin to process what Mrs. Wong actually said about last minute script changes and everything being a mess, and it's like someone from the lighting department is holding a bulb over my head and the switch inside me flips. This might just be my chance to turn everything around. I grab the garment bag I am holding a bit tighter and follow the clicks of Mrs. Wong's heels down the hall to the set.

CHAPTER 43

My heart is racing as I get to the thick double-wide doors that keep the soundstage protected from the idle chatter in the hall. I make sure the light that shows they are shooting is not on and grab the handle of the door. Even though it is as heavy as a wall, I pull it open like it's a tab on a can of soda. I think my adrenaline has kicked in.

It's a circus. Well actually, the set is still pristine but what is happening around, over, and next to the set is total chaos. People are arguing and waving their arms wildly. I see Mrs. Wong and she is calm and collected, while everyone else around her is losing their mind.

In the middle of it all, I see Phoebe. She has her head down and is looking at a script on a clipboard. Her mouth is open and it looks like she is trying to sound something out, but I am not sure what she is actually doing.

The wardrobe rack is behind Mrs. Wong, who is talking with some of the producers and other men in suits who must be the clients for the commercial. I decide to deliver the garment bag right to the rack so I can overhear any useful pieces of gossip.

As I get closer I can make out what at least one of the producers is saying. "No, no, no," he says, shaking his head. "We can't fix this in postproduction. Her lips won't match the words. It will look like a Godzilla movie. We don't want that!"

Hmm. So something is going on with the script and the live recorded sound, but what? I hang the garment bag on the rack but pretend to smooth it out, so as to keep myself within earshot.

"Well," Mrs. Wong says. "That's it then. She will have to do the tagline on camera in Chinese!"

I look over at Phoebe. Her eyes grow wide and she looks terrified, like she is about to go down the steepest drop of the world's tallest roller coaster.

"C'mon, Mrs. Wong," says a different balding executive in a suit. He has sweat covering the top of his head and looks like he has just been released from being trapped in a mine shaft. "Be reasonable. The kid has been struggling with this all morning. Give her a break. We can just dub it."

Mrs. Wong sweeps her hand across her body and waves just one of her perfectly manicured fingers at the sweaty guy. I can see the sweat drip from the top of his head to his face and down his nose. "Listen to me," she says in a voice so forceful every single person on the soundstage stops what they are doing and turns to hear what she will say. "My family's business is synonymous with the word *quality*—from Tokyo to Taipei and around the world. I will *not* compromise on quality. Never. Spa Girl will do it in Chinese!"

The place is silent.

Then she says, *"Shi shang wu nan shi . . ."*

And before she finishes I chime in with, *"zhi pa you xin ren."*

I know this expression very well since they used to say it all the time at school in Hong Kong. The teachers used it to encourage us to work harder. It's an old Chinese proverb that roughly means the same as the English expression "Where there's a will, there's a way." It's certainly a motto I take to heart, and, for the first time since Judith called to tell me I did not book the lead, things are looking up. I think.

Mrs. Wong looks at me and I give her my most innocent smile, making sure I exude confidence and charisma. "I have an idea!" she says. "I need producers and the director to meet with me. Everyone else take five. And I mean five!"

This is it. This could be it. There is no way they are going to let Phoebe ruin the commercial with her broken Chinese. Mrs. Wong is a smart business-woman. She knows I can at least get through simple Chinese after living in Hong Kong for a year. After all this, I am finally going to become Spa Girl. I should be jumping up and down in the air, but for some reason my feet stay planted firmly on the ground.

"Hey, Brittany," someone says while tapping me on the shoulder.

I am so confused by the recent turn of events and that I might actually book the Spa Girl role I don't even realize someone is calling my name. It's Martin—the production assistant who signed me in this morning.

"What's up?" I ask.

"There is someone in craft services who has been waiting to see you and, since she called five, I figured now would be a good time. I'll call you back over the speaker when we need you."

"Oh, okay," I say.

I walk out of the soundstage, figuring it's probably

best if I stay away from it while they decide whether or not they'll give the spot to me.

I walk down the hall to the other end of the building where the craft services tables are set up for lunch. I have no idea who could be visiting me on set, but I assume it's either my mom or my dad here to check up on me since they knew I was pretty upset about everything. Wait until they find out I might not have anything to be upset about anymore.

CHAPTER 44

I open the door to the craft services area and there he is.

Liam!

I've been so caught up in the shoot and being on set and Mrs. Wong and my last chance to actually become Spa Girl that I haven't had a chance to even think about him for the past few minutes.

Liam is standing in the back, away from the crew, with his back toward me. Before I let him know I am here, I just study him for a second. His head is tilted up toward the monitor and his hair is sticking up in spikes and tufts in a totally random, but adorable, style.

I realize his silhouette looks like an anime character, and it reminds me of that day on the train when he stopped to get a manga and we spent the whole ride home talking about drawing. That was only a few days before I hatched my plan. Before my desire to get "back on top" suffocated any real feelings I had.

Things seemed so much simpler back then. I thought I knew exactly what I wanted, but now, watching Liam from behind, I'm not so sure.

I think for the first time the only reason I want to book this spot so badly is because booking spots has been the only thing in my life I have ever even thought about wanting. I didn't even think I *could* want something else until I started taking art class and hanging out with Liam.

Liam must sense I am standing a few feet away from him because he turns away from the monitor and we are suddenly facing each other. "Wow!" he says, shaking his head a little. "I almost didn't recognize you."

What is he talking about? I was only in wardrobe and makeup a few minutes ago. I should be looking my best. I glance at myself in the reflection of the window just behind him. I look how I always look before a shoot: camera ready.

"Well, it's me," I say quietly, raising my shoulders.

"Well, sort of . . ." he says, giving me a sly, flirty smile. It's become harder and harder to resist his charm. "It's the *you* in all those commercials. I came to see the real you—the stubborn girl from art class with the wicked sense of humor and incredible talent for drawing. You know, the REAL Brittany Rush."

I don't respond.

I am, for the first time in my entire life perhaps, speechless.

I know people use that expression a lot, but in this moment, I am finally finding out what it truly means to be speechless. It means I am inside my head thinking about what Liam has just said to me and time has actually paused for a moment. It feels like the world has stopped spinning, because, he's RIGHT!

I always thought the girl in commercials was me. That we were the same person. After all, she looks so much like me and acts a lot like me. But the truth is, she is nothing like me.

She's a photocopy of something. There is nothing real about her. I'm beginning to think the real me is that girl from art class.

"I've got a present for you," Liam says, and he holds up a large, flat, square object wrapped in sparkly silver-and-purple paper that looks like a midsummer-night sky. I look at the beautifully wrapped package and want to tell Liam that just his being here has already given me a better present than he could possibly imagine. He goes to hand it to me when the loudspeaker interrupts.

"We need ALL talent on set. All talent on set for lead blocking and casting changes," a static voice announces from a loudspeaker over our heads.

Casting changes? Suddenly I come up with another idea. But this one is not just about helping me. This one, if it works, will help everyone get not only what they want, but also what they deserve.

"Liam," I say. "I'll be right back. I have to fix something but I'll be back."

I race down the hallway back toward the sound-stage. I can make this work. I know I can. If they use me as Spa Girl it will mean I'll not only look like the jerk who stole the part from Phoebe, but I'll also be stuck doing all of the additional promotional work in the fall. It will mean additional photo shoots, sound looping, and maybe even in-person events— all things I used to live for.

Now all I want is to be able to sit in an art studio with a fresh set of pastels, a blank sheet of thick off-white paper, and, of course, Liam. I have to fix this.

I burst open the doors of the soundstage and Mrs. Wong is standing on set surrounded by the producers.

When she sees me, she smiles and says, "Darling, *gong xi*." I know *gong xi* means "congratulations" in Chinese so I can imagine what she is going to say next. "I have some absolutely wonderful news for you."

I know she is about to tell me I am Spa Girl but I actually don't want to hear it. I can't believe I don't, because only a few hours ago I wanted to hear that more than anything in the world.

I see Phoebe sitting away from the group in a chair with the script in her hand. It's clear she has been defeated and she almost looks like she is about to cry. Yesterday the thought of seeing Phoebe cry brought me great joy, but now it breaks my heart.

I quickly walk past Mrs. Wong and say, "I'm so sorry. I have to go to the bathroom. It's like an emergency." I continue walking across the set toward the bathroom, making sure to stop by Phoebe. I grab her hand and, thinking of a quick excuse, I say, "You know how girls always do this sort of thing together."

Phoebe is totally confused and just follows me out of the soundstage and into the girl's room.

I close and lock the door behind us. Phoebe is clearly about to cry and says, "Congratulations. I overheard them say they are going to give you the Spa Girl role because you can actually remember and pronounce the words. You deserve it."

"Phoebe, no I don't. I don't deserve it at all." If only she knew how much I don't deserve it. "*You* deserve it!" I tell her. "You deserve it because you booked it because you know how to be yourself on camera." I remember thinking of the person I am on TV as a photocopy of something real, and I realize that Phoebe books so many things because she is the exact opposite. What she brings to a booking is herself. Her *real* self.

"Now, give me that script! Phoebe, you were cast as Spa Girl and you will be Spa Girl." I take the page out of her hand and look at her lines. My Chinese is not great, but I can figure out the line they want her to say easily enough. *Che ga di fan hun hao wan* basically means "this place is really cool." But Chinese is complicated because it uses all these tones, so even though you might pronounce it correctly, if you use the wrong tone, you could be saying something like "My cat eats pancakes for dinner" or something equally as ridiculous.

"We only have a few minutes," I tell her, "so listen and concentrate."

I say the words in my best Chinese and tell Phoebe to repeat after me. She does and I suddenly realize why they think they can't do the commercial with her. It sounds like someone has just thrown a box of trumpets down a stairwell.

"Again," I tell her, hoping the repetition will help it sink in. It sounds almost exactly the same except maybe someone has thrown in a few wind chimes with the trumpets. Phoebe knows she sounds terrible.

"I can't," she says. "I just can't do it. It's too hard."

"Phoebe, 'can't' is not part of my vocabulary." I say the phrase again and she repeats it. It still sounds terrible. There isn't a lot of time, and then it suddenly comes to me.

"Phoebe, you are trying to say the words in Chinese." She nods her head slowly. "But what we need to do is sing them!"

I explain to Phoebe that Chinese is like a song. I tell her not to think of it as words, but as a melody, and then I spend a few seconds teaching her to sing.

She picks it up very quickly. After a few tries, it actually sounds at least like how I think it should. At the very least, it's a million times better than what she was saying before.

We walk out of the bathroom and back to set.

When we get there, Mrs. Wong says, "Brittany, I have something to say to you . . ."

"Thank you, Mrs. Wong," I say as politely as possible. "But I think Phoebe has something to say to all of you first."

I nudge her just a bit and look her in the eye and nod as if to say, *You can do it.*

Then Phoebe says, *"Che ga di fan hun hao wan."* It's not perfect but it sounds very good, and the group of producers behind Mrs. Wong cheer. Even Mrs. Wong cracks a smile.

"Well done, Phoebe," Mrs. Wong says with only mild skepticism. She looks around the room for a moment and then says, "I guess this means we can proceed as originally planned."

The stillness of the studio turns into organized chaos as everyone prepares for lead blocking. Mrs. Wong walks past Phoebe and says, "I guess you had a very good teacher." Both Phoebe and Mrs. Wong look at me.

"Don't look at me," I say. "I'm not Phoebe's teacher. I'm just her friend." I smile at Phoebe and, for the first time, I mean it. Phoebe and I are friends.

"Well, then she has a good friend in you. A very good friend indeed." Mrs. Wong walks off set and as soon as the sound of her clicking heels has faded, Phoebe hugs me.

"Thank you so much. She's right. You are a good friend, Brittany, a *very* good friend. Thank you."

"You're welcome," I tell her. "Now get over to lead blocking before they try to book someone else." Phoebe squeezes my hand and goes to her position in front of the cameras. I look on set for a second and realize I used to think that's where life actually happened. In front of the cameras.

I used to think it was the *only* place life happened, but now I know that isn't true. I check with Martin to see if I am needed on set and when he releases me, I race back to craft services where my actual life is waiting to begin.

CHAPTER 45

Liam is standing right where I left him a few minutes ago. He looks so handsome. He's holding the shiny wrapped package at his side. "So, what is this?" I ask. I genuinely have no idea what it could be.

"Open it and find out."

I tear the paper down the front of the package and there, staring back at me, is one of my drawings from art class. It's the one that Mr. Snyder complimented me on. The one that he looked at when he told me I could take his advanced studio class. It's the drawing that made me think I could give up commercials before this whole stupid spa campaign came along. I can't believe it. I can't believe Liam took the time to do this for me. He took a piece of *my* art and framed it. I just stare for a moment at the collection of lines and shapes I created.

"When did you do this? *How* did you do this?" I ask.

Liam sort of laughs and tells me I left the drawing behind in class that day and he brought it into the city and had it professionally mounted and framed. He was going to give it to me yesterday but the timing was all off.

I've never seen a drawing of mine displayed. Sure, they've been on a few refrigerators here and there, but never framed, matted, and preserved under glass. Seeing my drawing like this makes me see it differently. I always thought drawing was just a hobby and that being in commercials was my passion.

Maybe I've had it backward. Maybe commercials are just a hobby and *drawing* is my passion.

When I think about the times I was happiest this summer, they all involve drawing and art and . . . Liam.

When I think about the times this summer that made me the most unhappy and frustrated, they involved auditions and callbacks. I could never give up commercials completely, but I wonder if they could just be *part* of my life instead of my *whole* life.

I stare at the image I created in the frame. It looks so professional, mounted and under glass. I have a flood of emotion that is not entirely unfamiliar. For a second, I just let the feeling wash over me without trying too hard to identify it. But then, I recognize it. It feels a little like when I see myself in a commercial, but looking at my drawing is more than that. Much more.

When I see myself in a commercial, it's like seeing myself as someone else. Looking at my drawing is like seeing myself as me. I feel like I am actually seeing *me*.

"Thank you, Liam," I say softly. He probably thinks I am thanking him for the framing, but I am actually thanking him for so much more.

He says, "You're welcome. I just wanted to do something special. Brit, I don't always understand you. But you always seem to know what you're doing. That's what I like about you. You are totally yourself. I don't know anyone else like you."

"That's right," I tell him. "I'm just me." And for the first time, being *me* is exactly who I want to be.

Don't miss the second book in

COMMERCIAL BREAKS,

Picture Perfect

I pick up the dishrag on top of the stool, look at it quickly, and smile broadly, making sure my face is not turned too far away and that my eyes are not squinting. I look at the pert blond woman standing next to me and say, "Mom, you did it. You got those grass stains out of my cheerleading skirt."

Ashley, the pert blonde, picks up the water bottle on the stool next to her, smiles as broadly as I am smiling, looks straight ahead, and says, "I didn't do it. Nature's Way did it. And it didn't hurt the environment."

That's my cue, so I say, "Now that deserves a cheer."

I am about to actually start my cheer when from behind the camera Neil says, "Dang. This dumb camera has been giving me problems all day. Can you hold while I try to fix it?" And as if someone has pricked the surface of a balloon with a needle, our version of an ideal world immediately collapses. Our commercial audition has paused, and reality creeps back in.

I am not a big fan of reality. Why would I be?

In commercials I'm the captain of the cheerleading squad who lives in a immaculate suburban home and has a clean skirt without grass stains, a perfect routine, and a gorgeous mother who laughs and smiles on cue.

In reality my mom is a math professor who thinks prime numbers are fascinating, and when I auditioned for the middle school cheerleading squad last year I tripped over my own shoelaces, knocking down the school mascot so Marty Pinkerman's furry squirrel head rolled off his human head and across the gymnasium, ending up at Principal Conner's feet. Needless to say, I did not make the squad and have little chance of even being allowed to attend future cheerleading tryouts.

But here in the cramped casting studio, or in a commercial on TV for thirty seconds, my life is picture perfect.

Neil takes the camera off the tripod and starts

fiddling with it. "Sorry, this will just take a second," he says. Ashley and I both nod, and then she bends over into some kind of yoga pose that she say helps her focus. Ashley is my absolute favorite fake mom in the world. She has straight blond hair that just brushes her shoulders, a small, perfectly symmetrical nose, and bright blue eyes that dance when the camera is rolling. I met her during a shoot for a commercial for an office supply store about a year ago. I played the daughter who couldn't decide if she wanted a sparkly pink notebook or a glittery purple one. She played the mom who let me buy both.

My dad saw the commercial last week while he was waiting for a flight at an airport in San Diego, and he actually called me right from the terminal. Even though it was about two o'clock in the morning, I was thrilled to get his call, since I hadn't heard from him in a while.

Ashley changes her pose and stretches her arms toward the ceiling. As she arches her back, I notice that her necklace slides around and dangles behind her. I know she'll want to be camera-ready when we start rolling again, so I tell her about the runaway chain.

"Oh, thanks, Cassie," she says, coming out of

her pose. She moves the chain back to her chest, and I notice the necklace is actually a beautiful gold heart-shaped locket.

"That's so pretty," I say.

"Oh, this?" she says, fingering the jewelry. "Well, I got it at the place on Eighth Street next to the bookstore. I had to. Jennifer was wearing almost the *exact* same necklace when she booked that cat food commercial, and Miranda was wearing one in that car commercial, so now *everyone* is wearing them." She opens the locket and looks at the picture inside. "I guess something about this locket screams 'young mom.' I dunno."

Sometimes I forget how supercompetitive the "young mom" category really is.

"Well, it's pretty," I say.

"Okay," Neil says. "I think we're rolling again. Let's take it from the top."

In an instant we are back at it. I pick up the dishrag pretending to be my cheerleading skirt, and we run through the lines, this time without stopping. I do a short cheer and Neil yells, "Cut!" Ashley picks up her bag, and I grab my backpack, and we head out of the tiny casting studio.

The crowded hallway is full of fake moms

and daughters reading through the lines we just finished. We are each just slight variations of the other. As always, there are a few new faces among the crowd of the usual girls.

"It was great seeing my favorite fake daughter," Ashley says, and gives me a tight hug. I delight in the fact that she thinks of me as her favorite fake daughter, but whenever she says it out loud and hugs me, I get this terrible feeling in the bottom of my stomach. The truth is, sometimes I wish Ashley was my real mother and that I was her real daughter. I feel like a terrible, evil person when I think these thoughts, since my real mother is a perfectly normal, mostly average mom who, for some misguided reason, believes that what you have on the inside is more important than what you look like on the outside—which explains why her wardrobe makes her look like an extra for *Woodstock*, the movie. I give myself a mental slap across the face to try and shake these thoughts from my mind.

"It was great see you, too. I really hope we book this one together," I tell her.

"That would be fun," she says, pulling off the headband she was wearing during the audition, sticking it in her bag, and letting her bangs fall over her face. "I'm off to my Pilates class. See you around." She glides through the crowd and makes her way out of the studios.

I decide to fix my hair in the bathroom before my next audition. The casting office I am going to for my next audition shares a bathroom with a couples counseling office, and more than once I've had to deal with mildly hysterical women while I was brushing my hair.

I walk down the hall toward the bathroom around the corner. As soon as I turn the corner, I spot the one person I am trying to avoid.

Faith Willis is heading toward the bathroom from the other direction. I immediately stop and hope she hasn't caught a glimpse of me. Faith and I are always competing against each other for the same spots, since we have a similar "look," although I once overheard a casting director say that Faith is more "upmarket" while I am more "theatrical." I'm not really sure what that means, but it didn't exactly make my self-esteem leap in the air. I'm pretty sure Faith booked the spot for that new energy drink I had a callback for a few weeks ago, so I am desperate to avoid her.

Half the girls I audition with are supersweet and

make you feel like you are part of a very cool club, but then there is the other half, who turn every callback into a battle of epic proportions. Faith is one of the high commanders in their army. I turn away from the bathrooms and walk down the hall to the elevators, thus avoiding any contact with her.

I make my way through the crowd, and when I'm on the other side of it, I hear someone calling my name. I turn around and see my friend Phoebe and her brother, Liam. Phoebe and I booked a cereal spot last year where we played two friends gossiping on the school bus. Within a few minutes of meeting each other, we became real friends. Phoebe is one of those girls who is just super friendly and supportive. I think that's why she has been booking everything lately. You can't turn on the TV without seeing her smooth blond hair and sunny smile. I couldn't be happier for her. She comes over and gives me a big hug. Phoebe is a serious hugger.

"Hey, Phoebe. Hi, Liam. I just saw your Apple-Time commercial last night, Pheebs. That dress you were wearing is so pretty. I loved the lacy skirt it had."

"Thanks," she says. "I loved, loved, *loved* the way that dress looked, but even thinking about it hurts."

"What do you mean?" I ask.

"Well you only saw the front of it on camera. They bought the wrong size, so the back was cut open just before we started rolling and they held the thing together with pins and duct-taped it to my body. That's why you never see my back and only see my face in the mirror of the vanity. It looked beautiful but felt awful."

"That sounds terrible," I tell her, but I know last-minute fittings can be brutal. Then I remember that I have to get to my next audition "I've got to run. I'm late for an appointment at Mel Bethany's."

Phoebe and Liam look at each other.

"The Maryland Lottery spot?" Liam asks as I pound my fist on the down button for the elevator.

"I just came from there," Phoebe says. She looks quickly from side to side and then whispers, "RR was in the waiting area, FYI."

RR stands for Rory Roberts, the boy currently holding the number two spot on my Crush List. And since the number one spot has been held by Johnny Depp since I was, like, six, RR is really in the highest-ranking position any mortal human can have. The elevator doors open, and I thank Phoebe for the information before hitting the *L* button for the lobby and saying a small prayer for an express ride to the ground floor. I look at my watch and realize that I still have plenty of time to make my appointment. The question is, will Rory still be waiting for his appointment and will I get a chance to go to the restroom and fix my face before "accidentally" running into him? Just once I would like to book a spot with him so we could hang out on set together. We've been at a few of the same auditions recently, but that has barely given me a chance to have any substantial interaction with him. I do, however, see him in the Mega Motors commercial pretty often.

When the elevator stops, I quickly walk through the ground-floor lobby and push my way through the revolving door. It's a sunny May afternoon, but there is still a chill in the air. As I start walking toward Broadway, I feel my cell phone vibrate in my pocket. I keep walking and pull the phone out to look at the screen. It's my agent, Honey Arbuckle. I can't believe Mel has already called my agent to find out where I am when I am not even late, at least not yet.

"Hey, Honey," I say without slowing down. "I'm on my way to Mel's right now. Neil had a camera malfunction and the elevator took forever and—" Honey cuts me off before I can finish my list of excuses.

"Listen, kiddo," she says in a raspy voice that sounds like she started smoking when she was a toddler. "Don't waste your time. You've been pulled from the list."

Sometimes at the last minute a casting company will change the call because the client changes their mind. One minute they want redheads with freckles and the next they want Latina twins over six feet tall. It's part of the business, but since Phoebe just came from the call, that can't have been what happened. "I don't understand," I tell Honey. "They didn't change the breakdown?"

"No, kiddo, they didn't," Honey tells me.

"So why shouldn't I go to the audition?" I ask in confusion.

"All I can say is that I had to pull you from the list. I gotta take this other call. Your mom will explain the rest. I hope I'll talk to you soon. Bye, kiddo." Honey hangs up, and I am just standing on the corner of Broadway and Eighteenth Street with my cell phone up to my ear and no one on the other end. For a second I consider just showing up at Mel

Bethany's and pretending I never got the message, but I know a stunt like that will get me banned from the casting office for life. In my mind, I go over the conversation I had with Honey. I don't understand why I was mysteriously pulled from the list. Suddenly I remember a very important phrase Honey said that went something like, "Your mom will explain."

That can only mean one thing.

New girls.
Same academy.
And some serious drama.

Join the team at the Canterwood Crest Academy at

CanterwoodCrest.com

Only the best class schedule, ever!

- Watch the latest book trailers
- Take a quiz! Which Canterwood Crest girl are you?
- Download an avatar of your fave character
- Check out the author's vlogs (video blogs)!

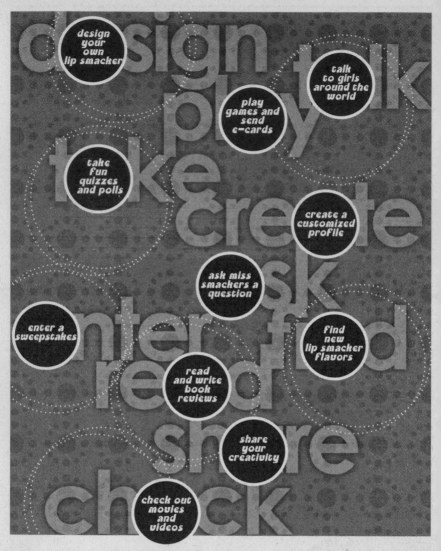

Jammed full of surprises!

LiP SMACKER.
L O U N G E

VISIT US AT WWW.LIPSMACKERLOUNGE.COM!

©2010 ASPIRE Brands, LLC

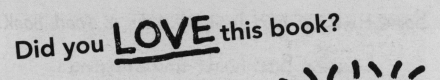